Lock Down Publications and Ca$h
Presents

I0666812

FO'EVA ROLLIN' 2

NO DISCIPLINE

Written By
Assa Raymond Baker

First Edition 2024

Printed in the United States of America

This is a work of fiction. Names, characters, places, and incidents either are products of the author's imagination or are used fictitiously. Any similarity to actual events or locales or persons, living or dead, is entirely coincidental.

Lock Down Publications
P.O. Box 944
Stockbridge, GA 30281
www.lockdownpublications.com

Like our page on Facebook: Lock Down Publications
www.facebook.com/lockdownpublications.ldp

Stay Connected with Us!

Text **LOCKDOWN** to 22828 to stay up-to-date with new releases, sneak peaks, contests and more…

Like our page on Facebook:
Lock Down Publications

Join Lock Down Publications/The New Era Reading Group

Visit our website:
www.lockdownpublications.com

Follow us on Instagram:
Lock Down Publications

Email Us: We want to hear from you!

PROLOGUE

Today was like every other day in House of Corrections. Dudes were sittin' around shit, talkin' about what they had and who they were on the streets. Actin' like life is one big muthafuckin' competition. I just shook my head at the F.A.N (Fake Ass Niggas). I had real shit on my mind. Hold up, let me introduce myself. My name's Daquan Walker aka, Soldier Bags. An' the only good thing this thug has going is that the relationship between me and my girl, Loni, is gettin' stronger. She even told me that loves me. We talked on the phone everyday and she get down here to see me twice a week. Loni's doin' her best to show me that I am not alone.

"Walker? Mail!" the deputy yelled from the officer's station. I got up and briskly, strolling over an' collecting my mail.

There were two envelopes, one from my lawyer and the other wasn't labeled. It has no return address whatsoever on it. I am curious but whatever it is has to wait, I opened and read my legal mail first.

Dear Mr. Walker:I'm writing to inform you that I've received all the Discovery paperwork. I now have all I need to prepare for trial. If there is anything you think that would help your case, please let me know. I'll see you after I've finished my review so we can go over our plan for trial.
Sincerely,
Anthony Scott

Alright, that's what's up. Now that he has the paperwork we can get this show on the road. The worse part 'bout this jail shit is the not knowing what's going on, especially when your future is in someone else's hands. But I got confidence in Anthony because Loni has confidence in him. I'm just not confident in the judicial system 'cause the great majority of men and women that holds a seat in the courts only see me as young black ghetto trash. Fuck 'em! They don't know my life. Anyway, lets get to this mysterious letter.

Soldier,

This is Chrissy. I'm not writing to ask how you doing or nothing because I don't care. I'm simply writing to say bye, bitch! Fuck you for everything that you put me through. I hate you! I hope you never get out. FYI nigga I'm the one who turned yo' punk ass in. You and Realla. And you don't gotta think about the baby because it's not yours. It's Maniac baby. Yeap, me and him been fuckin' pretty much since I started fuckin' with you. By the way, how did his dick taste? LOL! See you never, bitch ass nigga!Rot in there!

Damn! I ain't gonna lie I was kinda still in love with her, because she is or—well, was the mother of my child. But after reading Chrissy's letter, my heart broke and sank. Why would she do me like this? Why would Maniac be messin' with her behind my back. My whole world is fuckin' crushed, straight up. I'm sitting here questioning every minute of my life that I spent with them muthafuckas I called my friends and a bitch that I fuckin' fell in love with. They were the only ones I ever really trusted.

Maybe Assa was right: I am all I got. I know you don't know me or what happened, so allow me to vent and catch you up in the process.

Everybody got a story to tell
But I can honestly say dat I experience hell

5

I felt some pain as a kid
Dat had me ready to give
Until I met a group of kids
Dat had me ready to live
We got cool as the weather
Things turned out for the better
Started gettin' money together
We were robbin' whoever
But things started gettin' fishy
My girl started to dis me
The others started to spin me
And then they all were against me
I thought these guys were the coolest
But that was me thinkin' foolish I'm all I got...

Chapter 1

The brightly lit administration office was rather busy this morning. So much so that I was planning my escape. I can see it now: me running my ass off with the punkass security guards behind me sweating like the pigs they are, tryna catch me. But they can't 'cause I'm too fast for 'em.

"Daquan? Daquan Walker!" bellowed the wrinkled faced office assistant, snapping her fingers at me. "Get your head out of the clouds and go on in there," she said, snatching me back to reality.

"I hear you! Don't snap your fingers at me. I'm not a dog!" I retorted as I got up and perambulated in the direction that her lil fat finger pointed me in. It's only been approximately two hours after class started, and here I am already getting chewed out by the school's principal once again.

"Mr. Walker, you've given me no other choice. I'm giving you a three-day suspension for that little altercation that you were involved in," said Principal Winchester, her irritation with me clear as day in her voice. I said nothin'. Just sat there with my face scowled, staring at a red paperclip on the floor beneath her desk. "Mr. Walker?"

"What?" I responded sharply.

"If you keep this up . . ." She leaned forward on the desk separating us. "If you keep up this behavior I'm going to be forced to expel you from this school. This is an institution of learning, not a boxing ring!"

"So what! I don't like this school no-ways!"

The frustrated principal took a deep calming breath, at the same time massaging her temples, trying to fight off a headache before she spoke again.

"Is there something you want to say to me?" she asked on her exhale.

"No!" I shook my head so that she understood that no means *no*. I wasn't gonna apologize to her or anybody else.

"No?" she repeated, looking shocked by my answer. "Well, then you're free to go. I hope when you return you have a better attitude, Mr. Walker." She spoke to my back because I'd already grabbed my backpack and walked out of her office.

While walking down the corridors of the school, I could hear snickering an' whispering from the other kids as I passed them. I couldn't help but feel embarrassed, knowin' that I'm what gave 'em their giggles. That thought alone made me feel even more ashamed to be me. I dropped my head and picked up my pace, desperate to get out of sight and earshot of 'em all. Once I was out of the school building, I felt secure enough to pick my head up. The morning air was just starting to warm up; the sun felt good beaming on my face. Although the foster home where I lived is only five blocks away from the school, I had every intention on taking my sweet time getting there.

Dragging my feet, I reflected on the fight I got into in class so early in the day. I hated my life. I had no friends. I was the laughing stock of sixth grade, and to top it all off, I'd been separated from my real family due to child abuse and neglect. To be real, the home I was placed at wasn't much better. Yeah, I'd contemplated runnin' away so many times, but where would I go? An' how would I take care of myself? Before I could list more reasons to hate my life even more, I noticed the foster home had crept up on me. It was just three houses away now. I thought about takin' a trip around the block. I absolutely hated stayin' there, but being only twelve years old, I didn't have a choice.

Strolling 'cross the neatly cut front lawn, I went around to the back door. The front entrance was off-limits to me. I wasn't even allowed a key to get inside the house. I tapped on the door with my fist and waited. Before I could knock again, I heard the deadbolt locks on the door being twisted, and seconds later the door was snatched open.

"Boy, your school called and told me that you'd gotten into another fight and that you're suspended for three days. What's your problem?" My foster mom started scolding me before I could step foot into the house.

"He started it wit' me!" I exclaimed in my defense, an' she stepped aside, allowing me to enter the house. I'd almost wished she hadn't.

"I don't care who started it! You better start behaving, boy, before you end up in jail or dead!"

"I do be behavin'. Everybody there always messin' with me," I explained in a softer tone of voice.

"If them kids at that school pickin' on you, go tell your teacher. It's their job to make them stop, not yours."

"If I do that, then they ain't gonna do nothin' but mess with me even more for being a snitch."

"Well, you better start snitching or learn to ignore them, because if you get kicked out of that school . . . Boy, just— just go to your room. You're on punishment for two weeks!"

I nonchalantly headed down to the basement where my bedroom was. I didn't care about being suspended; I didn't like going to school anyway. An' being on punishment didn't bother me neither, 'cause it wasn't like I had a variety of privileges like other kids my age. I was limited to TV and outside. An' with no friends, I didn't go outside all that much. So since those are the only privileges I have to be restricted from, punishment was the least of my concerns. Being suspended was like a vacation to a kid like me, an' since the date was Thursday, I got five embarrassment-free days from that hell.

"Quan?"

9

I heard my foster mom yell from the top of the stairs.

"Yes, Mrs. Marshal!" I answered, dragging my feet over to the bottom of the stairs.

"Are you hungry?"

"A lil bit."

"Well, come eat this sandwich I made for you."

Thinkin' that this was one of the rare occasions that she was nice, I quickly made my way up the basement steps into the kitchen. She had a nice pastrami and Swiss cheese sandwich with a handful of plain Lay's potato chips on a paper plate waiting for me on the kitchen table. It was only after I sat down and took my first bite that I'd heard her yelling from the living room.

"Wash those dishes when you're done, Quan!"

I looked over at the sink and saw what looked like a hundred dirty dishes piled up. I wondered what had she been doing with her time. With a strong urge to refuse as my blood warmed, I somehow found the strength to hold my composure. I swallowed the food in my mouth, shaking my head.

"Yes, ma'am!"

Mrs. Marshal was a middle-aged, slightly heavyset, pretty-faced woman—the kinda female that you just knew was fine as hell when she was younger. Despite her warm and loving outward appearance of being a God-fearing woman, she really was borderline evil. Sometimes I would try to give her the benefit of the doubt and tell myself that she's only doing her job as a guardian. But whenever she did something nice for me, she followed it up with somethin' cruel, confirming my judgment about her evilness. Finishing my sandwich and chips, I tossed away my paper plate and got started on the pile of dishes. After about an hour of scrubbing the kitchen spotless clean, I dried my pruned, slaved hands, then went back down to my room. Exhausted, I stretched out across my twin-size bed and looked at the alarm clock sittin' across the room on the dresser. It read 4:11

p.m. The time made me think of Mr. Marshal. He usually made it home around 4:30. I liked him because he was a lot more patient with me than his wife, and a lot more understanding of my issues.

Before I knew it, I'd slipped into a comfortable rest, only to be disturbed by the sound of someone knockin' on my bedroom door. I sat up, slightly startled by the sudden noise, quickly glanced at the clock again, and found that what felt like hours of sleep was really only a little over 40 minutes.

"What's going on, D?" Mr. Marshal asked, walking over and sitting at the foot of my bed, lookin' like he was glad to be off his feet.

Even though his build was intimidating and he almost always wore a rough frown, I felt safe when he was around. Safe from criticism whenever I got in trouble, and he would just have a talk with me.

"Nothin' much. I got suspended from school today for fightin'."

"Yeah, I know. What happened though?"

I knew he was truly concerned, so I took a breath then began explaining my side of the story for the first time, because none of the teachers at school would listen and Mrs. Marshal didn't really care.

"I was in math class an' the teacher called me to the board to solve the problem that he'd put up there. I went, an' this dude yelled, 'Look at his shoes,' and everybody started laughin' at me. I kept my cool an' just focused on solving the problem the teacher asked me to. I did and went back to my seat. That's when the dude called me a bum. I called him one back, then he started talkin' 'bout my mama. Sayin' stuff like that's why she can't afford to buy me no shoes. Everybody started laughing harder, and the teacher was sayin' nothin' to 'em. So I got up and told him to shut up, an' when he got in my face I just started punching him in the face."

Mr. Marshal let out a chuckle, shaking his head.

"If I was you, I think I would've done the same thing. Why did you swing on him? Did he do something that made you feel like you had to take it there?"

"I don't know. It wasn't nothin' left to say, an' when he got in my face I figured that he wanted to fight."

"D, we can't solve all our problems with our fists. Sometimes you gotta ignore people. Now let me see what your shoes lookin' like." I got up and grabbed my black, well-worn Reebok Classics from under the bed. "Dang, them kicks busted!" he said, frowning. "Why didn't you tell me you needed shoes a long time ago? I'm going to take you to get some new ones on my next off day, but you gotta stay outta trouble. Deal?"

"Deal!" I agreed. Then he went back upstairs, and I heard him gettin' on Mrs. Marshal about not telling him about my shoes.

Chapter 2

Tuesday snuck up on me fast. I was having a nice dream about my perfect day out with my real family. In my dream, the weather was perfect, the water was fine; me and my five brothers an' little sister were all having the time of our lives at the Wisconsin Dells water park. In the dream, my mother even let her inner child out, racing down the water slide with me and playing all of the water games we could think of.

"Quan!" I heard my name being yelled, snatching me from my happy place. "Quan, are you ready for school?" Mrs. Marshal questioned, letting me know my little vacation was over.

"I'm up!" I responded as I glanced at the clock; it read 8:22 a.m. I'd forgotten to turn on the alarm, hell, I'd briefly forgotten about school altogether. I only had eight minutes to get there before the first class started.

"Well, you better start heading out before you're late. I'm not playing with you, Quan. You better not make me have to go out of this house to take you to school because you were late," she threatened.

I jumped outta bed and grabbed the first pair of jeans that my hand touched, then repeated that same process with the shirt. I threw them on with fresh socks and the same busted-up shoes, then rushed out of the house without brushin' my teeth or nothin'. I just didn't care anymore. The closer I got to the school, the more I remembered how much I hated it there. I looked down at my shoes—the same ones that I got in the fight over—and an anxious sickness turned my stomach. I could've kicked my own ass for not taking care of my hygiene before leaving the house. All I'd done was set myself up for more verbal abuse.

Arriving at the school, I instantly changed my mind about attending. I just stood there outside, contemplating what to do. There was no crowd out there that I could try and blend in with, so I went with my first mind and walked off in the other direction. Only, I didn't return to the foster home; I decided to just wander the streets 'til the end of the school day, then go home like nothin' happened.

Feeling like a genius, I walked to the park that was just 3½ blocks away from the foster home. I went and sat on the swing and began thinking of the dream I'd had before Mrs. Marshal's irritating voice woke me from it. I really missed my family. It had been approximately a year since I'd seen them, and not knowing when or if I would see them again was tearing me apart. Lost in thought, a few hours had passed with me still sitting on that swing. I saw a police van ride past. I thought nothin' of it until it made a hard U-turn and came in my direction. Not knowing what was going on, I just sat there watching it get closer to me.

A tall white male officer exited the van and approached me with his hand close to his gun.

"Hey, buddy, what's going on?" he inquired, sounding casual and friendly.

"Nothin', just swinging."

"Just swinging, huh? Why aren't you in school?"

"Because I didn't wanna go." The officer laughed like I'd said somethin' funny, then asked me my name.

"Daquan," I told him, watching him pull out a small notepad and write it down.

"Daquan, what's your last name?"

"Walker."

"What's your date of birth?" I told him it was 11/13/93.

"You got a birthday coming up in a couple of weeks, huh?"

"Yeah," I answered, smiling. Despite all my problems, I looked forward to my birthdays every year. I never got gifts or had a real party, but for some reason that day brought me great joy.

After the officer was done taking down my info, he casually informed me that I had to get up, turn around, and put my hands behind my back. I complied, then he said that he had to place me in the van until he got things situated. Again, I complied and was led to the rear of the van and helped inside. A short time later, the officer returned and informed me that he was taking me to the TABS center. I asked what the TABS center was.

"The TABS center is where we take kids that are truant from school until school is let out or your parent or legal guardian comes to get you."

"Oh," I said, relieved. I was thinking it was juvenile detention. Obviously, I'd never been, but I'd heard plenty of stories to know I didn't want to experience it firsthand.

We arrived at the Boys & Girls Club located on Sherman and Burleigh. The sight of the place made me think I was in for a good time. Once inside, the officer led me to a room where another officer awaited. He uncuffed me, and the other officer told me to go have a seat. I strolled towards the TV. There was a girl about my age and two boys probably a year or two older than me, sitting together and talking.

I sat next to one of the boys and stared up at the TV. Sitting on the other side of the boy I was next to was the girl, and beside her was the other boy. Even though I didn't give any of them eye contact, I could feel them lookin' at me. From my past experience with other kids, I thought better than to greet them.

"Aye, you?" Instantly feeling nervous for what's to come next, I looked to my left as the boy furthest from me asked, "What's yo' name?"

"Daquan," I answered, surprised, "but my momma 'nem call me Soldier Bags."

"Soldier Bags?" he repeated, sounding confused.

"Yeah, Soldier Bags," I confirmed.

"Like grocery bags?" he questioned again, still not understanding.

"Yeah, Soldier B-A-G-S, Bags."

"Why they call you that?"

"My momma said 'Bag' was the first word I said when I was a baby, and my brothers call me Soldier 'cause I like the movie *Rambo*."

"That was yo' first word?" he asked, sounding like I should've known something better to say as a baby.

"Yup!" I replied, and him and the others started laughing.

"Why you say 'bag'?"

"I don't know; I was a baby." They laughed a little more, which made me laugh. "What's y'all names?" I asked, feeling like it was my turn to ask questions.

"My name Lil Wes, my real name Wesley," the boy next to me said first.

"My name Chrissy," the girl followed.

"My name Maniac, my real name Jamiane," the last of the trio said, closing introductions.

"How old y'all is?" This time the smiley-faced girl spoke first.

"I'm twelve."

Maniac an' Lil Wes both told me they were thirteen, so for my final question I asked what school they went to. Before Lil Wes could answer, the black female officer sitting in front of the room called my name.

"Daquan Walker!" I spun around to face her. "Can you step up to the desk, please?" I got up and went to the desk, and she asked, "Is your foster mom Mary Marshal?"

"Yes."

"She's on her way to come get you."

"Okay," I said and walked off. When I got back to my seat, Lil Wes immediately questioned me.

"What she say?"

"She said my foster mom 'bout to come get me," I told him, rolling my eyes and huffing.

"Foster mom?" Maniac repeated.

"Yeah, my foster mom." I kinda felt embarrassed admitting that fact about me.

"You in a foster home?" Maniac asked, surprised, like he'd known me all my life and this was news to him.

"Duh, he just said his foster momma 'bout to come get him," Lil Wes spoke up, answering for me.

"Why you in a foster home?" Maniac questioned.

"I'm there because my real mom be beatin' on me and my brothers and my lil sister," I admitted, not ashamed or embarrassed to be tellin' them this.

"Daquan, let's go!" I heard Mrs. Marshal's angry voice demand from behind me.

"Bye, y'all," I said, sounding sadder than I meant to.

"Peace out, Bro," Lil Wes said.

"Bye, Soldier," Chrissy said, looking me right in the eyes.

"Peace, Bro," said Maniac.

As soon as I ambled over to the desk, Mrs. Marshal immediately went in on me.

"What's your problem, skipping school, boy?" she asked as she half-dragged me by my arm out of the room. I said nothing.

"Boy, you better answer me!"

"I don't wanna go to that school no more!" I answered with frustration in my voice.

"You better watch that tone, lil boy! And I don't care what you want and don't want to do. You're going to do what you're supposed to do, and that means go to school. You hear me?"

"Yeah," I answered just to get her to stop yelling at me in front of the other kids. It only lasted until we made it out to

17

the Boys & Girls Club's parking lot. I got in the backseat of the car, tunin' her out, and just stared out the window as she drove home.

Chapter 3

Once we were home, Mrs. Marshal sent me to my room. I laid in bed, not caring about Mrs. Marshal's attitude, and feeling grateful that I dodged another day of school. Just as soon as I got comfortable, I heard:

"Quan!"

I sat up frustrated, then I went to see what Mrs. Marshal wanted. When I walked into her room, she was sitting in a chair, watching *Jeopardy*. She looked at me and said:

"I don't know what yo' problem is, boy, but you better get it together. You making me look bad! Don't you ever pull no stunt like that again! You hear me?" I nodded yes. "Go to yo' room."

I walked out of Mrs. Marshal's. While passing through the kitchen, I swiped me a package of Pop-Tarts and rushed down to my room. There, I laid back on my bed, nibbling on one of the stolen Frosted Chocolate Pop-Tarts while thinking about the dream I was having earlier that morning. Before I knew it, I'd fallen asleep. I slept until late evening. When I awoke, I went to see if dinner had been made. Before I got to the kitchen, I smelled Mrs. Marshal's delicious home-fried lamb chops, which made my stomach growl.

"Have a seat, boy," Mrs. Marshal said when I entered the kitchen. I saw Mr. Marshal already seated at the head of the polished oak and glass dining room table and took a seat. Mrs. Marshal sat a plate in front of me containing two lamb chops, smothered mashed potatoes, and steamed mixed vegetables. Then she took her place at the other end of the table in front of her own plate of food.

"D, what happened to our deal?" Mr. Marshal inquired, breaking the awkward silence after saying grace over the meal.

"I don't know . . . I just got scared to go to school 'cause I knew everybody was gonna be talkin' about me."

"I can understand that. But man, you gotta ignore them knuckleheads."

"I do, but I be gettin' mad."

"You can't be lettin' them get to you. That's why they keep picking wit' you. Ya see, they know how to get to you, how to get a reaction outta you anytime they wanna good laugh. Just try ignoring them and see how it goes, okay?"

"Alright," I agreed.

"Now what's this business with you and the police?" he asked in between bites.

I briefly cut my eyes at Mrs. Marshal, swallowed the mouthful of potatoes, then ran the story of my police encounter down to him from the beginning. After dinner, I showered and headed to bed. It didn't take long for me to go back to sleep. This time, I awoke from a peaceful dream that had me feelin' depressed about not being with my family. I looked at the alarm clock on the dresser—it read 7:39 a.m. I got up and got ready for school.

I went in the bathroom, grabbed my toothbrush, and started brushing my teeth. I was just about finished when I caught a glimpse of someone walking past in the mirror. I looked out the door and saw it was Mr. Marshal.

"Let's have a good day today, D," he said over his shoulder.

"I will," I shouted in response as he exited the house. I got dressed, then went upstairs to grab me something to eat on my way out the door. Mrs. Marshal allows me to take a package of Pop-Tarts on my way to school, but sometimes I take two. Well, that day was one of those times.

I headed out the door and started walking to school. I ate the Pop-Tarts, anticipating what the day was gonna be like after not being there for six days. I ambled past kids standing on bus stops who all must've noticed my worn-out shoes because they all busted out laughing and giggling when I passed them.

I knew, as my anger started building, that no matter where I was, I would always be the ass end of everyone's jokes. My thoughts were racing with questions like: *Why are all the other kids so mean to me? Why don't nobody like me? How come I can't find a friend?* I wished that I didn't have to go to school; I hated everybody there. I wondered what schools did those kids I'd met at the Boys & Girls Club attend. They were cool. I wished I could hang with them again.

My thoughts were interrupted when I noticed that I'd arrived in front of the school. There were kids everywhere outside talking, laughing, and playing with each other. Witnessing that made me wish that I was invisible right then and there. I walked on with my head down, just enough for me to see in front of me as I tried to make my way into the school building.

"Where you going, bum? I bet yo' bum-ass goin' in there to eat breakfast with the rest of the bums!"

I turned around, and there stood Shawn, the boy that I had the fight with in class six days ago. Without responding, I turned back around and kept it moving. I was thinking of what Mr. Marshal had said about kids only messing with me when they know they can get to me. So I decided to listen to his advice and ignore Shawn. I didn't want to give him any more reasons to pick on me other than my clothes and shoes, so even though I liked the pancakes that the school was serving that morning, I didn't go to the cafeteria to get any as I'd planned on doing. Instead, I headed on to my locker.

"What's the matter, bum, you can't hear nomo?" Shawn and his lil' audience had followed me, laughing and teasing me.

I stopped in front of my locker. When I reached up to spin in the combination to unlock it—*Wham!* Shawn smacked my hand away. Now my blood was really boiling; this punk had put his hands on me. I dropped my head and took a quick moment to remember my promise. I slowly extended my hand again, and *Wham!* He slapped it away just like he'd done before. At this time, the bell rung, signaling classes were about to start. I held my breath and walked off, heading to class without putting my hoodie and backpack away.

"I told y'all he soft as cotton!" I heard Shawn saying, receiving more giggles from the instigators surrounding him. I thanked the good Lord that Shawn wasn't in my first-hour class with me. It gave me the time and space I needed to cool down a bit.

I was the first one to arrive to first-hour Social Studies class. I went straight for a seat in the back of the classroom. About thirty seconds later, the rest of the kids flooded into the room. A few of them had disappointed looks on their faces when they saw me sitting in one of the back desks. I didn't care—I was already having a messed-up day, so to hell with their feelings.

"You're in my seat, boy," exclaimed this girl named Michelle with a look of pure disgust.

"It doesn't matter where you sit, Michelle. Just have a seat," the teacher shouted, briefly pausing from taking attendance.

"Ugh! I hate him!" Michelle growled, stomping off.

I shyly surveyed the room, seeing quite a few disgusted stares directed at me. I folded my arms and put my head on the desk. I was just about angry at the world. Nobody was ever nice to me. Except for those kids I met at the Boys & Girls Club. Why couldn't I go to school with them? The sound of the bell snapped me out of my thoughts. I just about sprinted out of the classroom, heading to my locker to put my things away.

"Wuddup, bum!"

Without looking, I knew it was Shawn. I didn't want to bother with the punk, so I tried to keep it moving. That's when he shoved me in the back. I instantly spun around, my first thought being to swing off on him, but I thought better of it and attempted to walk away again. *Wham!* He punched me in the eye. Instantly, I jabbed him in the face three quick times, giving him the fight he didn't truly want. He stumbled backwards, a little surprised by my reaction like we hadn't just fought a week ago. He regained his footing, immediately swinging back. My vision was blurry, but I dodged under his wild fist, scooped him in the air, then power-slammed him on the hard floor. I pounced on him, feeding him vicious lefts and rights to his head, face, and mouth before springing to my feet and stomping. I kicked and stomped the punk until all of the teachers whose classes were close by showed up and pulled me off him. By that time, blood was everywhere, and Shawn just laid there deathly still with blood seeping from the back of his head and gashes in his face. As I was being hauled away, I heard people screaming, "Call the ambulance!"

Chapter 4

Yeah, so okay, I know I asked you to allow me to vent 'bout this shit, but I know you don't really wanna hear 'bout all my childhood tragedy or my juvenile delinquencies, so I'ma fast forward a bit. I need you to know everything I'd done for them bitches!

So this is years later, at approximately 11:00 p.m. The late summer air was warm enough to be dressed in only shorts and a wife-beater, so me and two of my childhood friends, Realla and Lil Wes, would've stood out dressed in the all-black jogging suits as we stealthily entered a shadowy gangway. We were all strapped for the occasion. I was carrying a pistol-grip 12-gauge pump-action shotgun, Lil Wes had a modified .380 auto with an extended clip, and Realla was strapped with his two Smith & Wesson .45 automatics. Whenever we went on moves, I always felt extra safer carrying the Mossberg—don't ask me why. But anyway, Lil Wes was the quickest of us all, so he always grabbed all of the valuables, and itchy-finger Realla was our shooter. He kept both pistols in his hands; if anyone moved the wrong way, he wouldn't hesitate to use 'em.

I hoisted Lil Wes up to the window of the house that we were in the gangway of so he could peep the scenery inside.

"What they doing?" Realla inquired, sounding extra anxious.

"They just sittin' 'round talkin'," Lil Wes answered.

"Y'all ready?"

"Hell yeah," both me and Lil Wes replied as I dropped him to his feet.

"Alright, let's go."

"Soldier, you go to the back door in case somebody try to run out that way—you can blow they ass back to the front," Lil Wes ordered.

"Fasho!" I agreed, briskly walking to the back door where I posted up with the Mossberg, ready for whatever and scanning my surroundings for any potential witnesses. Not long after I was in place, I heard a loud crash that told me they'd kicked in the front door. About 30 seconds later, someone was fidgeting with the locks on the door I was guarding. I placed my finger on the trigger, ready to blow at anybody who wasn't one of us. When it opened, I was relieved to see that it was Lil Wes letting me in.

Inside, we limited talking to help conceal our identities along with the masks that we had on. If one of us did talk, we used a Jamaican accent. And since I am almost flawless with mine, I usually did most of the talkin'.

"Wah gwaan?" I asked in patois. There were two frightened females in the place cryin' an' shit. The three dudes that were there just sat with their hands held high, lookin' goofy. "Where da bloodclot money?"

"Ain't no money! We ain't doin' nothin'!" a tall, dark-complexion dude exclaimed. The way he said it let me know he was the one in charge of the spot. I looked at him then pointed to Realla. "Yu, do 'im one." With the order, Realla marched over to him and slapped him with both .45s, one after the other. "Yuh tink mi come ere fa fun?" I asked, pausing for dramatics. "I'll ask yuh one more time, or erybody die, one by one. Where da bloodclot money?"

Boss man stared at me with a mug so mean. He had blood running down his face from the lil pistol-whipping he'd gotten. I glanced at the female beside 'im and noticed her unintentionally signaling with her eyes, by looking from me to the dresser. Even though this was usually Lil Wes's job, I promptly moved over to the dresser and began snatching out drawers until they all lay on the floor with the contents they once held. Lil Wes and Realla knew the drill and never took their guns off our victims.

That's when I observed a black metal lockbox sitting in the bottom of the dresser. I glanced over my shoulder at Lil Wes, then removed the lockbox from its hiding place and placed it on top of the dresser. Without losing sight of the vics, we swapped positions. Lil Wes instantly went to work on opening the cheap safe while I made the guys empty their pockets and stripped them of their jewelry.

"When we leave, nuh body move!" I threatened. Once we had all what we come for, the three of us quickly backed out of the busted front door one by one.

As soon as we were outside, we took off sprinting for the getaway car that Maniac was waiting for us in around the corner. When we reached the car, he had the doors unlocked and the engine running. With us all safely inside, Maniac peeled off into the night. Adrenaline pumping, we all broke into laughter.

"Soldier, you funny as hell. How you know the money was under the dresser?" Lil Wes asked.

"When I bluffed 'em out sayin' erybody gonna die, the bitch next to fam Realla split open told me with her eyes."

"Dawg, they was scared as hell!" Realla said, chiming in.

"How much y'all get?" Maniac inquired, turning south onto 27th Street.

"I don't know, but it look like a nice amount to split between the four of us though," Lil Wes replied, patting on his bulging pockets.

Not long after, we pulled beside Realla's Chevy Tahoe and ditched the stolen car we used for the caper. Oh, yeah— by the way, I'd started dating Lil Wes's sister, Chrissy, who was also a part of our crew. So we headed for the apartment that I shared with her. Chrissy was at work, so we all piled into the kitchen where we laid the money and everything on the table. The cash came out to a little over $15,500. Using a calculator to divide it equally, our cuts came to approximately $3,900 apiece.

With everyone satisfied and eager to go do whatever they had planned for their cuts of our take, they gathered their things then left me alone in the cozy one-bedroom apartment to wait on Chrissy to return. After tidying up the little mess the guys had left behind, I strolled into my bedroom, put the money and gold rosary in the drawer of the nightstand beside the full-size bed that I share with my first love. For some reason, I'm never really hungry after pullin' off one of our capers, so I just stripped out of the dirty jogging suit and hopped in the shower. About 10 minutes later, I was out of the steamy water, lying naked in bed with the 30-inch flat-screen TV on. I wasn't watching anything, just lying in the glow of the TV, reciting lyrics of a song I'd written in my teenage years. Sometime during, I'd drifted off to sleep.

Hard times got me stressin'
But I'm far from depression
I'm so humble they aggressive
Ain't no need for aggression
Think it's sweet 'cause my expression
I be leavin' 'em guessing
It's my G dat niggaz testing
Had to teach 'im a lesson
I swung like a pro and connected 'em all
Like the leaves in the autumn I was lettin' 'em fall
Now I'm sittin' in the box no regrets at all
'Cause some niggaz around here got no respect at all
Bet the next nigga check befo' he make a mistake
If he tryna get served I'ma make 'im a plate
I'm tryna do my time smooth 'til I'm out the gates
It's hard times in corrections when I'ma catch me a break

I was dreaming about fucking Cardi B when suddenly I'm awakened by Chrissy's warm, soft lips on my dick. I was pretty much used to her waking me up like that when she walks in and finds a clean home, plus money in the drawer. I grabbed the back of her head with one hand, letting her know I'm awake and that the drink she's workin' for is comin'. Not long after opening my eyes, I released in Chrissy's mouth. She thought I was done 'til I ordered her to wake my joint back up. Knowing what's coming next, she eagerly slurped it back into her mouth and went to sucking me better than the first time around.

When I was good and stiff, I pulled her up in the bed with me, flipping her over on all fours in one fluent motion. Before I slid inside her, I smacked and caressed her ass and enjoyed the view as it jiggled. She practically growled when I pushed inside her wetness. I hit her with hard, deep, long strokes. Then, moistening my thumb, I rubbed it around her butthole a few times before pressing my thumb inside. After a few more strokes, I replaced my thumb with my length. I could tell by the way her back arched and the way she clawed the bedsheets that she was loving every bit of it. Her freaky self began throwing it back at me as she looked back at me, and I almost lost it. But instead, I locked eyes with hers and I found that rhythm that made both of us cum. Chrissy collapsed, smiling and exhausted. I got up, went into the bathroom, relieved myself, and did a quick wash-up before returning to bed. I held her 'til we both fell asleep.

Chapter 5

The early part of the following day went pretty much how one would expect. Me and Chrissy woke up, had sex again, showered, dressed, and went out shopping together. Then she broke off from me to get her nails done or some shit before she had to go into work. So you know what I did. I linked up with my homies. After hours of doing nothing, one of 'em—I don't recall who—suggested we go to a house party. The party was set to start at 9:30 p.m.

At 9:15, Maniac, Lil Wes, Realla, and myself were riding in my Chevy Impala heading that way.

"Aye, Soldier, bro, stop and get some Loud," Realla shouted over the bass of the two 12-inch Pioneer subwoofers pounding the rapper, Tee Grizzley.

"From who?" I asked, turning down my radio.

"Dis one nigga on Burleigh."

"Burleigh? You fuck around over there?"

"Yeah, dude ain't off Burleigh though, he just live over there. Go down on 22nd," Realla directed.

We were already heading down Fond du Lac, so 22nd and Burleigh wasn't out of the way. I turned onto 22nd Street and slowed down.

"Stop right here!" Realla exclaimed over the radio again.

I immediately pulled over. The block was still pretty crowded with the hood's occupants. Everybody out there seemed to pause to stare at our unfamiliar vehicle. A lot of the neighborhoods in Milwaukee are territorial, hence the city's harsh nickname, Kilwaukee. Knowing this, we all placed our guns on our laps. The windows of my car was tinted dark so nobody could see inside, but better safe than buried.

"Hello! Yeah, I'm outside in the black Impala," Realla said into his phone, then ended the call. "He on his way out," he informed us.

Moments later, a short dude exited the gray house I was parked in front of and walked around to the passenger side of the car. Maniac's window was slightly lowered, so he directed him to the back door. Dude got in, and Realla made quick introductions, then made the buy. Dude got out and went back in the crib. As we pulled off, the stares we were receiving from the hood's natives got more intense. They were tryna extra hard to see who's in the car. I ignored 'em and kept going.

The party was on the Eastside, so that's where I headed. Blowing Loud, I zoomed through traffic like a lunatic. When we pulled up to the party, it was already jam-packed. There were people standing all outside, smokin' and drinkin'. The loud, hype music had plenty broads bouncing their asses. We sat in the car for a while, enjoying the show and rolling up more of the weed.

"We can't go up in here gettin' caught up in these hoes and lose focus."

"Man, whatever, you just talkin' that shit 'cause Chrissy got yo' balls cuffed up!" Maniac teased, gettin' a chuckle outta the others.

"Naw, I'm serious, bro. Watch erythang without being obvious. I see it's a lotta niggas here that I heard holdin'. We can use this party to find our next vics."

We sparked two blunts and put 'em in rotation.

"Aye, another thing, y'all. Don't accept no open drinks in this mufucka, they be mickey'n mufuckas down here," Lil Wes firmly stated.

We finished the blunts and headed inside. At the door, we found out that it was a free party, which explained why it was so packed. We passed the living room scene; I wasn't interested in the dancing that was going on there. We made our way to the kitchen, where a big dice game was going on. Hoes were standin' around, lookin' their prettiest in hopes to catch 'em a boss.

"Shoot da $200!" the guy animatedly shaking the dice said.

"Alright, shoot!" replied another guy, tossin' a stack of $20 bills in for the fade.

Like I knew would happen, Lil Wes pulled some money out of his pocket.

"I say he hit fo' dis hundred?" he offered, waving the $100 bill until another player took him up on the bet.

The guy with the dice rolled 'em across the floor. They stopped on double four.

"That's point!" the guy that shot the dice exclaimed with a chuckle.

"Let me fade whoever shootin' next?" Lil Wes said, promptly scooping up the two $100 bills he'd won. With him in the game to see who's holdin' the most money, I leaned into Realla's ear and told him that I was going elsewhere to do some homework. He nodded his approval, and I walked off. There was more music coming from the basement, so I went down to check it out. The scene in the basement was more laid back. Everyone seemed to be just lounging around, smokin' and drinkin'. The lighting was dim, and the air was cloudy with weed and cigarette smoke. A female approached me and asked me who I'd come with.

"Nobody," I lied. "What's yo' name?"

"Loni," she replied seductively.

My first thought was to get away from the thirsty-ass thot, but I ain't gon' lie to you, she was gorgeous, and the instant spark made me wanna know more 'bout her. Ms. Loni's hair was in kinky twist braids, she had a flawless milk chocolate complexion and perfect size breasts. Her jeans hugged her thighs and hips, promising a nice rearview. To top it off, she stood 5'5"; I love a short woman.

"Who'd you come with?" I inquired, tryna think of a way to get a view of her butt without lookin' like a creep.

"Nobody. I know some of the people here though," she explained.

"I can't really hear you. Wanna go upstairs where we can talk?" Loni nodded yes. "You can lead the way," I encouraged her. She walked in front of me, looking over her shoulder with a little smirk, knowing that I was checkin' her butt out. When we reached the kitchen, I saw Lil Wes was still shooting dice with Maniac watching over him. Realla had disappeared somewhere, most likely doing his homework. Finding a quieter place, I leaned against the wall and resumed talkin' to Loni. "So where you be at?"

"I'm from here on the East," she stated proudly.

"Aw, yeah? How long you been over here?"

"All my life. My whole family off the Eastside."

I felt my phone vibrating in my pocket and retrieved it. I saw it was a text from Maniac that said, "Let's go. I seen enough." I looked at the beauty in front of me, and there was that spark again. I asked for her phone number.

"Yeah, are you gon' really call?"

"What makes you think I won't? I wouldn't be leavin' you if I didn't have to go handle somethin' right quick."

"I don't know. You just look like a playa."

I laughed and handed her my phone. She put in her number and handed it back, taking herself a hug before walking off. I couldn't help but smile as I briskly walked off in the opposite direction. Outside, I spotted Realla standing a few feet away from the car. This was odd because I hadn't parked in front of the house party. I didn't want anyone to pay attention to who was getting in and out of my car. I strolled over, remotely unlockin' the doors. Once there, we slid into the front seats. I sent a text to the others that said,

"Ready." A few moments later, Lil Wes came outta the party, and shortly after, Maniac.

"So what's going on?" I inquired as soon as we were all in the car and pulling off. "What y'all see?"

"Man, I got hit for $400. Them hoe-ass niggaz was lockin' the dice. I ain't trippin' though, I'ma get my shit back and some," Lil Wes said, putting emphasis on the "some."

"Yeah, I seen that fool in that Robin jeans fit cuff a fat-ass knot. Him or the two niggas wit 'im ain't catch me lookin'. I ain't see 'em touch the dice, but they were dressed fresh," Maniac excitedly added.

"They did shoot. I kept goin' back and forth with that one nigga on side bets, but dude in the Robin fit shot a couple of times," Lil Wes corrected.

"I must've been on IG when that happen," Maniac admitted.

I stared at him through the rearview mirror and shook my head.

"See, ya slippin', bro. Shit coulda went down in that lil time," Realla told him.

"I got my cannon ready, my nigga. I ain't goin'!" he replied cockily.

"A mu'fucka can't tell you nothin', huh?" I chimed in, irritated by Maniac's carelessness.

We put together a plan where Lil Wes and Maniac would stay at the house party, watchin' the targets, and me and Realla would steal a car in preparation for our getaway. After discussing things, I dropped the two of 'em off a block away from the party. Then me and Realla rode deeper into the Eastside, lookin' for an easy vehicle to steal. Usually, the other two were the car thieves, but tonight we were trading places due to the fact they knew who the targets were and we didn't.

We approached a Dodge minivan. Driving slowly past it, we checked for a club or alarm. We didn't see neither, so we drove to the next block over, parked, grabbed two hooded sweatshirts out of the trunk, and strolled back to the minivan.

"You got the flathead?"

"Yeah, it's right here," I assured him, grabbing the screwdriver out of my sweatshirt pocket.

"You want dis one or do you want me to take it?"

"Don't matter to me."

"Give me the flat and grab that brick off that step right there."

I gave him the screwdriver, then passed him the brick. He began popping the lock on the driver's door. I kept watch with my hand on my banger for any wannabe heroes. I heard the door open and rushed over to the passenger door while he pounded the screwdriver into the ignition, popping it out. Seconds later, the minivan started up. I jumped in and we pulled off, heading back to my car. Realla pulled up beside it. I got out and into my car immediately, calling his phone.

"Wuddup, bro?"

"I'ma trail you so the police can't get behind you. You just find somewhere close to the party for me to park my car so we could ditch that steamer and make a clean getaway."

"Got you!"

As soon as we hung up, I called Maniac's phone.

"Yo?" he answered.

"What's shakin'?"

"Shit, man, chillin'. Nawl, I ain't come wit' nobody. I'm by myself."

"Awe, we on our way. Y'all meet us around the corner."

"Shit, man, I might leave in a lil bit. Cuz, I'ma holla at you." The way Maniac was talking let me know that our targets was close enough to overhear him.

Realla found a discrete spot not too close or far from the party, and pulled over. I parked my car there, got out and popped the trunk. I grabbed the other two hoodies for the others, some gloves, then got back in the steamer with

Realla. When we were half a block away, I texted the others to meet us.

Chapter 6

When we were all together again, Lil Wes told Realla to pull a little closer so we would have a better view. He did, and we began our stakeout for the targets they'd chosen. We didn't have our masks, so we took our t-shirts and covered our heads with 'em so all that could be seen was our eyes. With faces covered and dressed in black hoodies, all we had to do was pull the hoods up, and we were good to go. The back windows of the minivan were tinted but not the fronts, so to avoid being seen, me and Realla reclined our seats. After about twenty restless minutes, Lil Wes spotted his targets.

"There they go right here," he exclaimed excitedly, tapping on me and Realla's shoulders.

I glanced at the time on the dashboard; it read 11:42 p.m. Then I watched three nicely dressed guys pile up into a custom-painted red Audi A8.

"Aw, these niggas gotta be holdin', ridin' in somethin' phat like dat," Realla said, eyeing the car.

"We sure 'bout to find out," I replied. The Audi made a U-turn, now heading in the opposite direction from us. Once it was down the street, Realla made a swift U-turn, following them. "Don't let them get too far away."

"How you wanna do it?"

"Stay close but not too close. When they stop for a red light, bump they car—you know they gon' get out running they mouth, and that's when we pounce on 'em."

Realla chuckled his agreement to my suggested plan. It just so happened they were approaching a stop sign. The Audi eased to a stop, but Realla didn't until the van collided with the car's bumper.

"Man, what the fuck!" the driver of the Audi snapped, hopping out, followed by his guys. As they advanced on the minivan, me, Lil Wes, and Maniac jumped out of it, guns trained on 'em.

"Lay da fuck dow', pussyclot!" I ordered in a shaky Jamaican accent. By the time I got the word *clot* outta my mouth, Lil Wes and Maniac were attacking the vic's pockets. "Nuh move a bloodclot muscle." The three guys were frozen by shock and surprise. After relieving the trio of their valuables, Lil Wes and Maniac took the vics' phones, smashing them on the ground. "Lay ya pussy asses down and face da oddaway!" I shouted.

With no other choice, they reluctantly complied. We got in the van, and Realla peeled off. Before we reached the middle of the next block, we heard gunshots. I looked in the sideview mirror and saw the red Audi on our tail. The passenger's arm was hanging out the window with a gun aimed at us.

"Aye, them niggas bussin' at us!" I yelled. Before I could say anything else, the back window imploded, spraying us with glass. Maniac snatched the sliding door open, returning fire. "Aye, head towards my car and let Lil Wes nem out. Then try to shake them mufuckas so we can jump outta this bitch somewhere!"

"Alright."

"Don't let them out right by my shit."

"Nigga, I know! Shoot back or something, I got this!"

Surprisingly, the minivan had a nice distance in front of the car. When we were close enough to my car, Realla slowed down, and Lil Wes and Maniac jumped out, sprinting. I sent a few shots at the Audi in hopes that it would follow us—and they did, still shooting at us. Storming the minivan through traffic, Realla did his best to avoid us getting killed by taking corners sharply, smashing down alleys, running red lights, and whatever else, trying to lose the hostiles. My phone rang, and I answered it.

"Where y'all at?"

"Nigga, where y'all at?" Lil Wes countered.

"We by the BP gas station on Keefe."

"Alright, here we come."

"Aye, stay in this area so Lil Wes nem Maniac can catch up," I told Realla.

After bending a few corners, my Impala appeared behind the Audi with Lil Wes hanging out of the window firing at the car. The Audi swerved but kept coming. Lil Wes fired another three shots to the back of the Audi; this time, it swerved out of control, jumped the curb, and crashed into a light pole. When we saw the collision, Realla continued storming the van until we were about a mile away from the scene. The harmonious sound of police sirens told us it was time to ditch the van. Realla pulled into an alley, and we left the van running and got in the back seat of my car.

"Man, that shit was wild right there!" I said excitedly as Maniac casually drove away.

"Yeah, dem niggas didn't let us take they shit easily," Realla said, pulling the shirt from around his neck.

"Shit, a nigga can't do nothin' but respect 'em for that," I said, doing the same. "Aye, how much did dem niggas have anyway?" Realla asked the others.

"Man, y'all ain't gon' believe dis shit. This nigga said he dropped the merch when we was runnin' to the car," Maniac informed us, sounding disappointed.

"What the fuck!" Realla exclaimed, surprised.

"What da fuck you mean you dropped the merch?" I calmly demanded an explanation.

"Bro, when I was runnin', I felt somethin' fall outta my pocket. With dem bullets flyin', I ain't think to go back and check to see what it was. When I got in the car, I checked my pockets to see what all I hit 'em fo' and the shit wasn't there," Lil Wes explained defensively.

"So, Maniac, what you get off them niggas?" I asked in the same frustrated tone.

"Nothing but some weed. I gave him the lil knot I took off fat dude before I found the weed on 'im."

"Yeah, y'all right, I can't believe this shit. Is y'all fuckin' around wit' us or what?" Realla questioned, hoping they were joking.

"Man, I'm serious!" Lil Wes stated.

"Man, I just got shot at, in a stolen car and some more shit, and y'all dropped da merch? Man, take me da fuck home!" Realla snapped, shaking his head.

"Calm down, bro, we ain't lost or gained nothing, so we good," I said to Realla, trying to relieve some of the tension even though I felt the same way.

"Nigga, what you mean we ain't lost or gained nothing? We clearly just lost what we gained! I don't do blank missions, my nigga, and I ain't no sucka!" Realla said with an implied tone.

"Nigga, what you tryna say?" Lil Wes inquired.

"Everybody know how this shit really went—four niggas go on a lick and two niggas ain't gettin' shit!" Realla retorted.

"Man, you tripping. We ain't never played each other on no moves," I stated before things could escalate.

"Man, I ain't tryin' to hear that shit! Let me out!" Realla demanded.

"Bro, chill, you tripping," Maniac said with concern.

"Dawg, man, I said let me out!"

Maniac pulled over and let Realla out of the car.

"You sure this what you wanna do?" Maniac asked. Realla started walking, which gave him his answer.

"Pull off, bro. I gotta get to the crib," I said, hurt by Realla walking off on us.

"You good, Bags?"

"What you mean?" I asked, questioning Lil Wes's inquiry.

"Is you trippin' over this lil shit too?"

"Man, I would love to have that paper, but I ain't trippin'. I trust you niggas."

"I don't know what yo' guy on," Maniac stated, quickly disowning Realla.

I blew it off and let him drop Lil Wes, then himself, off. Disappointed, I sent Realla a text asking if he was good, but he didn't reply, so I headed on home. When I got there, it was after 1:00 a.m., and Chrissy was asleep. I tried my best to quietly gather my things for a shower. When I was ready to get in the water, Chrissy had awakened.

"Where you been?" she asked, immediately getting outta bed.

"I was with the guys tryna do somethin'," I answered. She knows how we got money, so she knew what I meant.

"So did y'all come up?" she inquired in a softer tone.

"We did, but yo' brother said he lost the shit."

"You expect me to believe that shit?" she snapped.

"What?"

"You heard me, Quan."

"Where's this coming from?"

"What was you really out there doing?"

"Bae, you trippin'. Go back to sleep," I stated dismissively.

"I ain't trippin'. You the one trippin'! Coming up in here this late talking 'bout you was tryna do something wit' nothing to show for it. What bitch was you fuckin' with? Huh, tell me that!"

"What the fuck are you talking about?"

"I heard you was at a party all up in some bitch face."

"I told you we were on something!"

"How you on something talking to a bitch?"

"Man, who told you that anyway?"

"Don't worry about it. What you should be worried 'bout is where you gon' sleep tonight!"

"What?"

"You heard me, nigga. Go find that bitch at that party, and ask her can you stay with her."

"Chrissy, I pay bills around here too, I ain't goin' nowhere!"

"But yo' name ain't on no lease. So bye!"

I stared at her for about five seconds, seriously contemplating smacking da shit outta her. But instead, I put my clothes back on, grabbed my keys and left.

Chapter 7

Know every experience's a lesson / Just study yo situation / And notice the hidden message / Make observation be yo finest profession / But taking heed that perception / Is to viewer's discretion / Don't be quick to open doors / Off impressive impressions / And even later down the line / You gotta keep second guessing / You might think they're not snakes / But they're the best at deceptions / Never let yo guard down / Sometimes be overly overprotective...

As I wrote these lyrics in my phone, I wondered if my best friends were really as loyal as they claim to be. My thoughts were interrupted by an incoming call from my Mama.

"Hello?"

"Boy, what's yo' problem callin' me at 1:30 in the morning?"

"Chrissy put me out again, and I was tryna get you to come open the door."

"Oh, y'all fightin' again, huh?" my mom asked, sounding annoyed.

"Yeah, you know how she gets."

"Where yo' ass at now?"

"I'm in back of yo' house sittin' in my car." I could hear her getting up and walking, so I assumed she was coming to open the door. I got out the car, armed the alarm, and walked to the house. My assumption was right; by the time I got there, she was unlocking the back door.

"Did you sleep in your car last night?" she asked, stepping aside so I could enter.

"Yeah, you ain't answer the phone, and I ain't wanna bang on the door that late."

"Boy, what's the difference between banging on the door and calling my phone? You still wakin' me up out my sleep."

"I dunno," I answered, asking myself why did I come over here?

"Well, while you here, I need to borrow some money."

"I ain't got no money," I stated, now really asking myself why the fuck did I come over here. "But how much you need?" I halfheartedly asked.

"How much you got?"

"I got a couple of dollars."

"What's a couple dollars, Soldier? Damn, boy, stop playin'!"

"I got like $300-some odd dollars, close to four."

"Well, let me borrow two of that."

I frowned at her request and asked her what she needed it for, while at the same time going in my pocket to retrieve the money.

"This rent coming up, and I ain't got it all. I really need more than two hundred, but I don't wanna leave you broke," she said, trying to sound sincere.

I knew she was lying by the aroma in her kitchen where we were. It smelled like every bit of crack, and by the look of her, I could tell she was back to smoking and needing another fix. But knowing I needed a place to crash and that she wouldn't hesitate the slightest to deny me shelter if I denied her money, I reluctantly gave her the $200.

"Where Tricc at?" I asked, wondering where my brother was while she in there getting high.

"He left sometime yesterday and ain't been back since."

I wondered what he was out doing. It would be a good guess that Tricc was somewhere thieving. Tricc's a hardcore thief. He didn't discriminate; he stole from whoever and whatever he set his sights on. On that thought, I went into the living room and stretched out on the couch, thinking about my girl. There's been times when Chrissy has gotten mad and put me out, but I couldn't understand how she could let something so petty come between us. Sometimes I wonder if we just need a break from each other. I've thought about leaving her ass a few times, but my heart won't let me do it.

Without realizing it, I'd dozed off, and not long after, I felt someone nudging my shoulder. When I opened my eyes, I saw my brother Tricc smiling at me.

"Wuddup, bro!" he greeted excitedly.

"Shit, man, wuddup wit' you?"

"Man, I ain't on shit. About to blow this Loud. You tryna match?"

"I ain't got no Loud," I stated, wiping sleep from my eyes.

"Put half on this shit then," he said, holding up a blunt.

I reached in my pocket for my cash, and finding it empty, I thought I was trippin', so I checked my other pocket, and all I felt was my phone. I got up and reached in the couch cushions only to find my car keys and some other miscellaneous coins. I immediately turned to Tricc.

"Bro, stop playin' with me."

"What da fuck you talkin' about?" he replied, frowning.

"Where my money at?" I demanded.

"Nigga, I dunno, you geeked!" he said, matching my tone.

I went looking for my mom.

"Mama!" I shouted, walking through the house.

"I'm in here!" she replied from the bathroom.

"Ma, come here!" I shouted, banging on the door. I heard the toilet flush, and then the door opened.

"Damn, boy, what?" she asked, annoyed, stepping out of a cloud of crack smoke.

"Did you go in my pockets while I was sleeping?" Her eyes widened with rage.

"Boy, don't you ever accuse me of stealin' from yo ass! You just gave me some damn money, boy. How you gon' accuse me of stealin'?"

"I ain't been sleep but a few minutes, and Tricc just got here."

"Boy, you been sleep over three hours, and Tricc got here a lil bit after you laid down!" she angrily explained.

I considered what she said and went to confront my brother again. When I got back in the living room, he was watching TV with an angry expression, smoking his blunt. Tricc didn't even look at me. Knowing that both him and my mom are stubborn and too smart to incriminate themselves—and for all I knew, they could've both robbed me—taking this all into consideration, I said, "Fuck it, y'all can have that shit!" Then I stormed out of the house and headed to my car.

The farther I got away from the two of them, the more I wanted to go back and solve the mystery, but once again, I knew I'd never get the answer I wanted. Madder than hell, I got in my car and slammed the door shut. A minute later, I remembered the emergency cash that I kept beneath the ashtray. Retrieving it, I stared at the $50 bill, angry at myself for letting myself get reduced to using it. I glanced at my rearview and saw Tricc strolling toward me. I quickly started my car and peeled off before he could reach the door.

I drove to the gas station and purchased $30 worth of gas. While I was pumping the gas, I checked the time—it was 10 a.m. I thought to myself, I could go for some McDonald's breakfast. With my gas hand reading almost full, I felt a little better knowing I had enough gas to get me around until something came up. I went to McDonald's and ordered a steak, egg, and cheese bagel, two hash browns, and some orange juice to wash it down. I was sitting in my car eating when my phone rang; I snatched it up, hoping it was Chrissy.

"Hello?" I answered, chewing.

"Wuddup, bro! What you on?" Realla inquired.

"Shit, finishing up this food. Why, wuddup?"

"Man, I need some money, like bad!" he stated. I could hear the desperation in his voice.

"I'm fucked up on cash, bro," I responded, not going into detail about why I was broke.

"Yeah, I kinda figured that. I know you was counting on that lil move last night too."

"Yeah, that shit was fucked up," I retorted, voicing my disappointment.

"I don't wanna talk about that shit again though. Check it out. I got somethin' for us right now."

"Yeah?"

"Yeah, just me and you though," he said seriously.

"What you mean?"

"Just me and you, not them other niggas."

"Why not though?"

"Man, you in or out?" he demanded.

"Uhh, I'm in. Where you at?"

"I'm at my grandma house down the street from yo' crib."

"Alright, I'm on my way." I ate my food on the way to Realla's grandmother's house. When I got out front, I called him.

"Yo?" he answered. I told him I was outside. "Here I come now," he said, ending the call. After about 5 minutes, he came outta the house, got in the car, and immediately greeted me with our signature handshake.

"Where was you at?" he asked.

"McDonald's."

"Awe, you ain't tell them niggas, did you?"

"Naw, we good."

"Aw, I asked 'cause I walked down there and seen Maniac's car but not yours. I ain't knock on the door because I ain't tryna see them niggas just yet."

"I ain't even been down there since after the move. Chrissy put me out last night."

"For what?"

"Somebody told her I was fuckin' with some bitch at that party, and she ain't believe we went on a move."

Realla began shaking his head and said, "Mu'fuckas need to mind they business."

"It's what it is. What you got for us though?" I asked, getting back to business.

"My auntie fuck with this nigga who be servin'. The nigga got hella cake. And we ain't even gotta poke 'im; we're just breakin' in the crib."

"You don't think that shit gon' come back to you?"

"Shit mu'fuckas be runnin' in and out they crib all the time. I wish that bitch would blame it on me."

"You sure you wanna do this?"

"Hell yeah. I'm positive!"

"What all he got in there?"

"He sell Loud and White so I know he got somethin' for us. I'm hoping he got a stash spot somewhere in the crib."

"When you tryna do it?"

"Shit, right now."

"Where they stay?" I inquired while pulling into traffic.

"Over on 19th and Hampton."

On the way to the spot, I decided to pick Realla's brain about the situation that went down between the four of us.

"Man, I hope we come up good outta this. Some crazy shit been goin' on all around me," I said, sparking conversation. I was looking out of the corner of my eye at Realla's reaction.

"Bro, tell me about it. My car actin' funny, my bitch actin' funny." Realla paused, scoffed, then added, "Niggas acting funny."

Right then I took advantage of the opportunity to see where he was at with the whole situation from the other night.

"What you talkin' 'bout bro?"

"Man, between you and me, them niggas ain't lose no merch like that that easily. Lil Wes too money-hungry. I think they played us. Stop actin' so naïve, my nigga. Every time dem niggas need somethin', you there, but dem niggas don't never got yo' back like you got theirs though. Then they quick to scream that we all we got shit to make us feel like they a hunnid percent. Something funny be up with them niggas, bro. And they be usin' us like a muthafucka."

"I hear you, my nigga," I retorted, taking everything he'd said to me into serious consideration.

Chapter 8

As instructed, I turned onto the block of 19th and Hampton. Almost immediately, Realla pointed me to a nice white house with black trim, medium-sized.

"Is that a duplex?"

"Yup, but the neighbors downstairs ain't never home. If they are, fuck 'em. We just gotta move fast."

"Okay then, we in and out that bitch!" I agreed as I sped off, looking for a place to park.

"Pull in the alley so won't nobody really see us."

I chose the alley behind the spot and parked two houses away in front of a garage. Then I retrieved my gun from beneath my seat where I put it before going in my mama's crib. Realla always carried, so I rightfully assumed that bro was strapped. We put on our hoods to conceal our identities some, then got outta the car.

We crept through the gangway of the houses, checking our surroundings for witnesses like we always did. Finding the coast clear, we began looking for a way inside. The spot was on the lower level, so that made it a little easier. Realla suggested a window on the back of the spot.

"Come on, I'll lift you up so you can see if you can open it without making all that much noise," I said, then hoisted him up. Not long after, I heard the window open, and I pushed up to help him through.

"I'll open the back door for you," he assured me before disappearing.

I jogged to the back door and impatiently waited for it to open, and after about 30 seconds, I was inside. We ran up the few steps leading from the back door into the lower unit. Since Realla didn't know anything helpful about the spot from the door, we split up. I went into the bedroom closest to me and searched it. I mean, I thoroughly searched it—I flipped the mattress off the bed, I dumped out the dresser drawers, making sure to search beneath it and inside the closet. Disappointed with the bedroom, I went into the kitchen and decided to search it since I had to pass through it to get to another room.

Starting with the refrigerator, I went through the freezer, searching open boxes of popsicles and *Hungry Man* meals. Finished there, I rummaged through the cabinets. Beneath the kitchen sink, I found a solid block of weed. Now, I wasn't the best at eyeballing weight, but I knew it was more than a quarter pound. I excitedly stuffed it in my hoodie, then moved to the bathroom. Right away, I found a small black and gold gun safe stashed behind the medicine cabinet. I figured it had to be the boyfriend's stash. I took it, then went to find Realla.

When I stepped into the room where my partner was, I found him in a small rage, ripping through things like the Tasmanian Devil. When he saw me, he said, "Bro, I can't find shit! I found a couple dollars, and that's it."

"Check it out!" I showed him the box and said, "This here probably what we came for. You tryna hit it?"

"Hell yeah. We been in this bitch too long."

With that being said, we both dashed for the back door. On our way out, we heard the elderly neighbors coming down the backstairs. Before they could spot us, we pulled our shirts over our faces and picked up our pace. Once out the door, we ran through the gangway back to my car, jumped in, and peeled off. Realla sat beside me in the passenger seat, dialing numbers into the keypad of the safe, desperately tryna find the right combination to unlock it.

"Man, I hope we hit the jackpot with this!" he excitedly exclaimed.

"What combination you trying?"

"I'm trying they birthdays and shit. Ain't none of it working."

"It's probably his mama's b-day or they anniversary or some shit like that."

"We don't know none of that, so we gon' have to break this muthafucka open."

"That was my idea anyway," I added, and we both laughed.

We posted up in back of Realla's grandmother's house and thought of ways to get in the safe. It was nice and sturdy, so he suggested using a flathead screwdriver. Realla dashed to the back of my car and got it outta my trunk. When he came back, we both took a shot at prying it open with no luck. We tried everything, even getting out and slamming it on the alley floor. Nothing worked.

"Bro, let's go to AutoZone and rent a crowbar. I bet that'll work," I stated, wiping sweat from my face.

"Man, that ain't nothing but a bigger flathead. What makes you think that's gon' work?"

"Man, it's worth a shot. Let's go." We got back in the car and took off to AutoZone. When we pulled up in the parking lot, I thought about all the little money that I had on me and said, "Bro, that muthafucka better have some cash in it, 'cause I'm broke as hell."

"Damn, man, I almost forgot about this money I found." Realla admitted, immediately pulling the wad outta his pocket and counting it. "This sixteen fifty."

"Shit, I can work with that."

"Hell yeah, nigga, me too!"

"Don't forget that weed back there I found," I said, pointing to the backseat where I'd tossed it and our hoodies.

Realla spun in the seat, snatched up the block, and happily sang out, "I got the feeling, ooooohhh!" We both laughed at his singing. Now $825 richer, I strolled into AutoZone to rent a crowbar. I got back in the car, handed the tool to Realla, then pulled into the alley behind the auto parts store. Realla set the safe on the ground, and I jammed the crowbar in the crack of the box and pried with all my might. It took me a while, but it popped open.

Both of our eyes lit up when we saw what was inside. There was dope, some cash, and a gun in it. Realla snatched everything up and quickly hopped back in the car before anyone seen it. I zoomed outta the alley and parked a few blocks away. The first thing we did was count the money. It came out to $8,000 in mostly small bills, but we were content with splitting it.

I scooped up the bag of pills to get a better look at them and saw they were Oxycodone. My mother instantly popped to mind. As far as I know, she never used prescription meds to get high, but she has friends that did. While I thought on it, I picked up one of the four equally sized individually packaged balls of cocaine that Realla was holding along with the Glock 23, smiling.

"What you thinkin'?"

"I know who'll buy this gun and dope right now," Realla stated, pulling out his phone.

"What about the pills?"

"Hello?" Realla said into his phone. "Where you at?" he continued. "I got somethin' for you. I'm on my way."

"Where we going?" I asked.

"On the Southside," he answered, still smiling.

"Where, and what you up to?"

"28th and Lincoln. I ain't up to nothin', just go, damn!"

I drove along 27th Street and crossed the 27th Street bridge.

"Hey, what we gonna do with the pills?" I inquired again.

"You always lettin' people make decisions for you. What you wanna do with 'em?"

"This was your move, my nigga."

"You found 'em though. See, my nigga, you're too nice. That's why muthafuckas be gettin' over on you."

"Whatever! Alright, fuck it! Let's keep 'em and sell 'em ourselves."

"Bet, divide them up," he said. "Bro, remember what I said, don't tell Maniac and Lil Wes about this."

"I got you, bro."

"Cos you know Maniac's pops be fuckin' with my auntie's boyfriend, and he might pull some foul shit."

"Aw yeah, fosho."

"Don't even let 'em know you holdin', 'cause you know somehow, someway, it'll get back."

"Alright, man, damn!"

"I'm just makin' sure we on the same page so you won't be blind to shit and do some shit."

The south side of Milwaukee is like a different state. Entering it from the north side of the city, you're enveloped by its Spanish community. That changes when you get further into it, but we were right where we wanted to be. When I reached Lincoln Avenue, I turned right, then made another right on 28th.

"Slow down, I gotta remember the house," Realla said, already calling the expected buyer. "Hello? I'm outside, bro . . . Alright." He ended the call, then said, "Right here, here it go," pointing at a yellow and white cottage-style home. I pulled over, and about 5 minutes later, Realla's phone rang again. "Whuddup? Yeah, I'm in the black Impala . . . Bring a scale too," he instructed before ending the call. "He say he on his way out."

"Cool," I replied. When I looked to my right, I saw a black dude approaching my car. I clutched my gun and unlocked the doors for him. Realla told him to get in the back seat.

"What you got for me?" he asked, right away handing Realla a compact digital scale.

"This here." Realla pulled out one of the balls of coke and put it on the scale. The coke weighed 29.4 grams. "You see this a lil over a ounce, so what's its worth to you?"

One thing I learned long ago about selling things is to never ask the buyer what they'll give you for what you're selling. It lets them know that you don't know the worth of what you have. The guy asked to see the dope; with no hesitation Realla handed it to him. Dude opened it dipped his finger in the bag, then rubbed it on his gums.

"Man, lil bro, this shit weak as hell! But I'll give you a couple bucks for it still since you came over here," he said, trying to sound convincing.

"Man, hell naw! I had some action blow some of dat shit so I know that shit good. I ain't going, my nigga!" I responded, pretending to be offended. Realla was shocked by my outburst but didn't protest it.

"Aw, this yo' shit?" the guy inquired.

"Yeah!"

"Well, what you want for it?"

"I'll let you get it for eleven hunnid."

"You can't go down on it?" he negotiated.

"Go down like how much?"

"Let me give you, like, seven?"

"Man, hell naw. I'm good."

"What's the lowest you'll go."

Seeing how bad he wanted it let me know it had some value to it.

"Man, the lowest I'll go is 9 hunnid since you Realla's guy." My bluffing worked, he agreed to pay the $900.

"I got this too, KD," Realla spoke up, revealing the gun.

"Damn, what you want for that?" he asked.

"I need like a nickel fa him, no bullshit."

"Man, you lil niggas breakin' me." He chuckled. "Let me give you 350?"

"Just 'cause you the big homie I'll take it."

"Alright. I'll be right back with y'all bread."

As soon as KD was out of earshot, Realla busted out laughing.

"Soldier, you fuckin' snapped! You made it sound like you be out here trappin fo'real. If you ain't let muthafuckas walk all over you, you'd be deadly out here." Realla complimented me.

Chapter 9

KD returning to the car interrupted the heartfelt discussion we were having about me standing up for myself. As soon as KD's butt touched the seat, he was handing us each the money we had agreed to with him. Satisfied, Realla gave him his purchases. But before KD got back out, I showed him the rest of the coke.

"Man, ya see I got that shit. When you need some more, just hit bro line, but this here is the last 'til I re-up in a few days," I baited him.

"Shit, let me buy two more off you then?"

"Check it—add three mo' hunnid to it and I'll let you owe me on the last one?"

"A nigga would be a fool to pass that up," Realla added.

"Man, you lil niggas broke me and made me rich at the same time," KD said, shaking his head. "Being all the real with you, I ain't got an extra three unless I give the banger back," he cut his eyes at Realla.

"Don't look at me; I need this lil change to get my whip fixed. Big bro, I know you good for it. Soldier, I vouch fo' 'im," Realla said, tossing the ball back in my court.

"Say no mo'." I agreed, and KD made a mad dash back in the house and was back with the rest of the agreed cash in a flash. This told me he was being honest about not having all the money. Realla handed him all three ounces.

"I'll be hittin' y'all in a minute!" he promised, concluding our business with a handshake.

It was pure coincidence that when I pressed play on the radio, the song *Sold Out* by Yo Gotti pounded out of the speakers. We sped away feeling good. At the corner, Realla suddenly muted the music.

"Aye, pull up to El Rey's on 14th and Forest Home so we can sit and divide this bread up."

"How you know the South Side so good?"

"When I'm not with y'all, I be fuckin' with these hoes over here. I love these Latinas. I'm weak fo' a lil Mexicana. They call ya 'Papi' while you beatin' up they guts," he explained.

"Shit, put me in with one, my nigga!" I exclaimed excitedly. He laughed and said he got me. "Now show me where the fuck I'm goin'."

Realla turned back up the music and started pointing out directions. Before I knew it, we were in front of El Rey's. I found a place to park on the lot and pulled out the money we'd accumulated and divided it between us. I let Realla have the odds since I knew he had to get his car fixed. It felt amazing holding all of that money after losing everything hours earlier. Now all I needed was a shower and a change of clothes.

"What we gonna do with this weed?" Realla asked.

"We keepin' the shit!" I replied with authority. He liked my answer because he replied with a huge smile.

On our way back to the North Side, I stopped at a gas station and picked up a scale for us to weigh the weed on.

"Hello? . . . Alright, here I come!" Realla shouted into his phone. "Bro, drop me off at the crib," he told me, sounding irritated. I asked him what was up. "My bitch trippin' and shit."

When we got to his house, Realla put a wad of cash in his girl's hand and sent her into the bedroom while we sat at the dining room table weighing the weed. Once we had it all divided up, I took off, leaving him to deal with whatever his girl was pouting about. Back in my car, I placed the pills and $1,000 in my stash spot, then headed back to the gas station to get me something to drink and some wraps so I could roll me a nice blunt of the weed. That's when I observed a police car pull into traffic a few cars behind me. It was pure paranoia that made me make the sudden turn at the corner to avoid them, but when I checked the rearview, they were turning right behind me. I instantly panicked, stomping the accelerator to the floor; and the chase was on.

I had a little lead on them, so I hit a corner where there was a lot of guys posted out on the block. Thinking quickly, I started flinging the weed out of the passenger window, praying that the guys would snatch it up and run. In the rearview, I saw that my prayer had been answered. The loss hurt, but easy come, easy go, right? I should've also asked for the police to catch a flat tire or something because they caught up to me quick. I hit another corner and had to slam on brakes, barely avoiding colliding with a big moving truck that was double-parked, blocking the street and my chance at escape.

"Driver! Shut off the car and get out slowly with your hands up!" the cops commanded, both of them using their car doors as shields with their guns trained on me. I complied.

"Slowly walk to the back of the car and place your hands on the trunk!"

I thought about running, but there were too many kids outside, and I didn't want to risk getting them or myself shot by a trigger-happy cop, so I did as I was told. That's when the officer snatched my arms behind my back, cuffed me, then brutally slammed me to the street for no reason.

"He's not resisting! You don't gotta do him like that!" I heard people yelling at the police.

"What's dis shit about?" I asked as the officer let me up and sat me on the curb while the other searched my car.

"Whose car is this?"

"It's my girl's car. We share it."

"Really? This car is reported stolen by the owner."

"What da fuck!" The news shocked me. I couldn't believe Chrissy had done that. I knew for sure that I was going to jail when I saw the second officer holding the gun and some weed that must've fallen on the floor for me to have missed tossing it out with the rest of it.

"Are you going to own up to this or try to put it off on the owner?" he asked, waving the contraband in my face.

"Yeah, whatever," I stated defiantly. With that, I was stood up and patted down.

"Whoo, lookie here! You out here hustling good, aren't you?" The officer's voice was full of sarcasm after pulling the cash out of my pockets.

"I don't hustle."

"Yeah, right, and I'm not a cop." They both laughed, then put me in the back of the squad car where they ran my name. I heard the officer standing outside of the car call Chrissy and inform her that he had found her car. He told her where to pick up the keys and where the car would be parked if she couldn't make it there within the next half hour. Another police car pulled up to be nosy and offered to wait there for her, so the officer turned over the keys to them, and off to the precinct I went.

Chapter 10

My precinct stay wasn't long, but it was uncomfortable. I was glad when they told me I was being moved to the County jail. But the Milwaukee County jail's booking room was even more uncomfortable and crowded. After having my mugshot taken and being fingerprinted, I was sent out into the holding area, where I was harassed by the other inmates for my cold bologna sandwiches. The only good news I got out of all this was that Chrissy wasn't pressing any charges. I don't see why she would call the car in stolen in the first place. Yeah, her name was just on the title, but I bought it.

With that out of the way, I was now only facing misdemeanor charges of carrying a concealed weapon and possession of a controlled substance. Feeling a little better, I called it a night. As soon as I started nodding off, I heard an officer yelling my name. When I looked up, he instructed me to come up to the red line. I did as I was asked and stood with a few others that the officer had also called.

"You guys are going upstairs. When we get to the other side, grab a bag and have a seat on the bench. After I take down your bag number, give me your clothing size, and I'll get you a change of clothes. After you change from your personal clothing into the bag, we'll grab your linen, and I'll take you to your assigned housing unit. Understand?" the officer announced. We all agreed, and he took us single file to the other side, where we did everything he said we would do. Once everyone was ready, he led us into a hallway containing four elevators. "Walker, you'll be going to Pod 3C, cell 9," he announced, and we all boarded one elevator. We reached the third floor, and he told everybody to get off.

Other than me, there were five dudes. Three were coming on the third floor with me but to different pods, and the other two were going to the fifth and sixth floor. The C.O. escorting us took the three dudes coming to the same floor as me to the left. When the officer returned, he walked me into Pod 3C. The pod looked a lot like the detention center, only bigger, and it was painted mostly yellow like the door. The lights were dim, and everyone was locked in.

"You're going in cell 9," the officer reminded me.

I looked at the numbers painted on the doors until I found cell 9. When I found it, I walked towards it. The officer went behind the desk and popped it open. This was my first time in the County jail, but it felt as if I'd been here before. When I entered my room, there was someone in there. He was laying down on the bottom bunk, but he looked up when he heard the door pop open. He didn't say anything, just turned over and went back to sleep. I just put my sheets and blanket on the top bunk and didn't even bother to make the bed because I was so tired. I just climbed up and dozed off.

When I woke up in the morning, it was because a female officer was at the door demanding me and my cellmate show her our wristbands. We both got up and walked to the door. My cellmate didn't have a shirt on, and I understood why. Our cell felt like an oven. The officer then demanded we stand outside our door like everyone else. I slid on my shower shoes, then stood outside the door. It felt like all eyes were on me. I scanned the room, looking at all the unfamiliar faces. My celly pulled the door closed, and seconds later, I heard the toilet flush.

"That bitch a crank, bro. You better make yo' bed before she do her round," my celly informed me, keeping his eyes on the cute officer.

"Alright, good lookin' out," I responded. I made my bed pretty fast and was back at the door before the officer made it to the center of the day-room.

"My name is Officer McCoy. Y'all know my expectations, and if you don't, then here they are. No fighting, no flooding, no loud noise in the day-room, only four at a table, no cell visiting, and stay off the top tier if your room is not up there. Walker, Hall, and Baker, you guys have court today. You come get your trays first."

Me and the other two guys called walked over and got our breakfast trays. When the two inmates handing out milks and trays handed me my tray, I couldn't help but think, *What the fuck is this?* Breakfast was a biscuit, some gray gravy-like substance, and what looked like some dry-ass scalloped potatoes. I sat down with the tray and just stared at it.

"You don't want that, bro?" some guy who looked about my age asked me.

"Hell naw."

"Can I get it?"

"Come get this shit," I responded. He threw up his index finger, telling me to hold on.

"Bottom tier, come get your trays!" the female officer shouted. The guy who asked for my tray took off for the breakfast line. When he got his tray, he sat next to me and slid my tray towards him.

"Walker, Hall, Baker, your ride is here," Officer McCoy shouted.

We all headed to the unit exit, where a male officer waited for us. When we got down to court staging, the officer told Hall and Baker they could stay there and that I was going to intake court. He escorted me in another direction than the other two guys.

"What's the difference from where I'm going and where they going?" I inquired.

"They been through intake already."

When we got to our destination, he put me in a cell with two other guys. There was a white guy and a Hispanic guy in the room. The white guy spoke up as soon as the door closed to the room.

"Hey, man, do you know what they'll do to you for a DUI?"

"Naw, this my first time in the County," I confessed.

We all sat quietly until they buzzed the door and had us all come out. A bailiff walked us to a bench and chained one of our wrists to it. The first to go in was the white guy. He came out moments later, saying he was going to lose his job if he didn't get out that same day. From the look in his eyes, he was on the verge of crying. Next to go in was me. The bailiff strapped a Velcro belt around my waist with some handcuffs attached to the front of it. He walked me into the courtroom and sat me next to an older white guy with silvery grayish hair and glasses.

"I'm your public defender. My name is Toby Sanchez. How you doing today?" he introduced himself, covering the microphone on the table in front of us.

"I'm cool."

"Good," he said, taking his hand off the microphone.

The court magistrate began talking and reading off my charges. There was another white guy at a table on my left who said he was representing the state of Wisconsin. My PD introduced himself to the court and said he was representing me. After all that, they came up with a bail for $5,000 and another court date for a preliminary hearing. My heart sank. I wasn't sure if my homies would come get me for five grand. I didn't have anybody else to turn to. My public defender looked at me and said he was going to try and get back into court later that day or tomorrow for a bail reduction. I was outraged. I felt like screaming or even crying.

The following day, some guys on the pod were sitting around a table sharing some of their personal music with each other. One of them asked me if I could rap.

"I be tryin' sometimes."

"Man, I know you can rap. You got music notes tatted on you an' shit. Come spit that shit," he said, pointing to my arm.

"Man, I'm not that good." I wasn't being modest, but I'm always my worst critic when it comes to my music. I just didn't feel I had the skill, but it was something I liked to do.

"I just wanna hear somethin', bro. You good," he said, still trying to get me to rap. I caved in and moved closer to the small crowd, and I gave myself a beat by pounding on the table. Once I found the rhythm, I began my freestyle.

It all started / With bein' broke / Winter time with no coat / In a trap house with no dope / On the verge of lost hope / I knew I had to make somethin' happen if I wanted to live / But my options were limited / I was just a kid / I'm done playin' / Fuck it I give up on God / My plan though is to steal and rob / All I need is my pistol and a bitch that mob / If you don't wanna be a target den stay outta my way / I'll give you clips like a movie / I'm talkin' play by play . . .

When I stopped, they all had surprised looks on their faces, and they were smiling, giving me credit.

"What kinda music you make?" this guy asked me.

"I usually just stick to shit I been through."

"Do you be going to the studio out there?"

"Hell naw, I just be writing shit in my phone. I don't even make hooks for 'em."

"My niggas got a studio, and they only charge $20 an hour."

"Where at?"

"In the hood on 39th and Cherry."

"I might have to check that muthafucka out."

"It's the white corner house, right on 39th, with the brick porch. What's yo' name, bro?"

"Soldier Bags. My name Soldier."

"Soldier, my name Mack, bro," he told me while offering me his hand. I shook it, and that's when the officer called my name.

"Walker? Walker, you got an attorney visit!" McCoy informed me.

I got up and walked to the desk, and she instructed me to go out to the floor control desk, saying they'd give me further instructions there. When I got out there, a heavyset Spanish female officer led me to a room in the hall. The conference room contained two chairs and a table. I sat in one of the chairs and impatiently waited. A few minutes later, Toby Sanchez came in.

"Well, I got you a bail reduction and a PR bond. Do you know what that is?"

"Nope."

"That's when the court plays your bail. You should be going home today or tomorrow." I felt a surge of excitement flow through my entire body. All I could say at the time was, "Okay."

"Okay, you still have preliminary court in a few days, so make sure you show up on time."

"Alright, thanks!"

"No problem, man. You take care."

"I will. You do too, man!"

"Will do."

I went back to the pod gassed up.

"What happen?" Mack asked.

"My public defender said I should be going home today or tomorrow. He got me a PR bond or something like that."

"Awe, you good den, fool."

Later that night, I was called for release.

Chapter 11

The big steel security door leading to the lobby hadn't slammed shut behind me before I'd ripped open the clear plastic property bag that contained my shoestrings, cellphone, and a few other miscellaneous items of mine.I retrieved my phone and called Realla.

"Hello?" he answered on the on second ring.

"Dawg, what's good, bro!"

"Nigga, what da fuck happened to you?"

"Man, long story. Did you get yo' car back working?"

"It's in the shop now, but I'm in my girl whip right now. Why, what up?"

"I need you to scoop me from the county jail."

"What da! . . . Alright, here I come, bro."

"Aye, I'ma be walking up Highland. I ain't tryna be standin' 'round outside this bitch." He promised to be on his way, then we ended the call and I got to marching West up Highland Boulevard. Realla must've been in the area because I'd only gotten about five blocks away before he'd pulled up beside me. I haven't seen my homeboy in three days. I was geeked to be free. I got in the car smiling from ear to ear.

"Damn, nigga, you stank!" Realla shouted, cracking the windows.

"Man, I don't even give a fuck! I'm just glad to be out that bitch," I retorted, smiling.

"Now what the fuck happen to you?"

"Dawg, man, soon as I dropped you off, the police got behind me. You know I had all that merch with me, so I took 'em on one. I hit a block with a bunch of niggas outside an' got to tossin' the weed outta da window while still driving. In all that I didn't see one of the packs fall back in the car, so when I had to pull over . . ."

"Nigga, why you had to pull over?"

"Aw, it was a big ass truck blockin' the whole street when I bent the corner. I was stuck like Chuck." I shook my head. "Anyways, the police said Chrissy's bitchass reported my car stolen."

"Man, you bullshittin'!"

"Bro, on my mama! And on top of that I got knocked with the heat and that weed that fell out. They took my money on some punk shit. It wasn't even mentioned at court."

"Dat's that bullshit!" Realla exclaimed, shaking his head. "So what now?"

"I don't know. You think you could let me get a shower and something clean to put on?"

"Yeah, I got you." He went to his grandmother's house; there, I showered and changed. He gave me some new underwear, socks, and a black Nike sweat suit. "You gon' go see what up with Chrissy while we over here?"

"Yeah, I'ma walk down there. You ain't talked to Lil Wes and Maniac?"

"Yeah, they hit me up. We ain't kick it though. I told 'em I was busy with shortie."

"Aw, okay, I'm about to head down there." With that said, I headed down to Chrissy's. It no longer felt comfortable saying our place after what she did to me, and her talking that shit about my name not being on the lease. I couldn't help but feel anxious on my way down there. I was trippin' about our relationship. She'd called the police in the past to have me removed from the house, but reported the car that I bought stolen. That was crossing a line. But she didn't press charges on me, though, and that's what's what was causing my confusion.

When I got to the corner of the block, I immediately spotted Maniac's car parked out front of the building. I called his phone to see what was up and got no answer. Curious, I went to the back of the apartment building, and I found my Impala parked in its slot. Since Chrissy didn't like to drive, it was where it should've been. I called Lil Wes's phone and didn't get an answer either. I didn't call Chrissy because I didn't wanna talk to her. I just wanted to get my shit and go. The rear entrance door of the building was always open, so I proceeded inside straight to the apartment.

Standing outside of the door, I heard talking and laughter. I knocked on the door because my key is attached to the keyring that my car keys are on. I heard feet shuffling and then Lil Wes asked who is it.

"Soldier!"

"Who?" he asked like he couldn't believe what he had heard.

"Soldier!" The door opened and he stood there with a blunt in his hand.

"Dawg, wussup!" he greeted, reaching out for a handshake.

"Shit, wussup wit' y'all?" I asked halfheartedly shaking his hand, then walking and and closing the door behind me.

"Shit, my nigga, we been low. I heard yo' ass went to jail?"

"Man, hell yeah! That was some bullshit. Where yo' sister at?" I asked, taking the blunt from him and sitting down beside Maniac on the couch.

"She at work. Why you go to jail?" Lil Wes asked.

"She reported the car stolen but didn't press charges on me. But I got knocked with my heat and some weed."

"Damn, on what! She told us she reported the car stolen because she was salty at you. We ain't know you got pinched with some merch," Maniac said, looking up from texting on his phone. I took a pull of the blunt and let the smoke settle real good before I blew out the smoke.

"Man, hell yeah. I was callin' y'all phones and y'all wasn't accepting my calls."

"We was gettin' calls from the jail an' figured they were from you, but our phone wouldn't let us accept none of 'em," Maniac explained.

"How much weed you get pinched with?" Lil Wes inquired.

"Like a QP."

"Damn, where you come up with that from?" he asked, surprised by the amount.

I remembered what Realla said about not telling them about the move we pulled. I realized then that I should've said less so they wouldn't be curious. I came up with a lie right away.

"I stole it from my mom's crib. I took a nap on her couch and somebody peeled me for the couple dollars I had on after I loaned my mom two hundred. I didn't know who it belonged to but I took it since couldn't nobody tell me who peeled me."

"Damn, yo' people stay gettin' over on yo ass," he said with a chuckle.

"You got some cash on you now?" Maniac asked.

"Naw, I'm broke as hell, they took my money," I admitted, then they both went in their pockets and pulled out some money and handed me $250 apiece. "Where y'all niggas come up at?" I wasn't all that curious, just wondering why the kindness, and happy that I wasn't flat broke anymore.

"The lil bitch Keke I fuck with cashed me out, bro. For no reason, she just called me and told me to come see her. When I got there, she laced me with some dome and a few gees." Lil Wes boasted.

I didn't know Keke all that well, but I knew she wasn't exactly financially stable. Lil Wes was the one who's usually giving her a few bucks here and there. I knew he is in love with her but let him tell it she was just another fling.

"That's from all the times you looked out for her. That shit finally paid off." I joked.

"Nigga, fuck you!" he retorted, laughing.

"Man, I need to bust a power move," I said, getting serious.

"Why you say that?" Maniac asked.

"I gotta buy a car, I need a heat, and I need some cash left over to live on."

"Muthafucka, you got a car!" Lil Wes exclaimed.

"Man, that muthafucka in yo' sister's name. Ain't no tellin' if she gonna pull that shit again with me. Or even put me out again."

"Well, fuck whatever she on. You know we got yo' back, my nigga," Maniac promised.

"Yeah, we all we got, fool!" Lil Wes added. Hearing them say that made me feel better about my situation.

We sat in the living room smoking and talking about old times and fantasizing about the future until I fell asleep on the couch. I woke up to the smell of Chrissy cooking. The living room and the kitchen were almost connected, so I could see everything she was doing. Quickly scanning the place, I saw that Lil Wes and Maniac were nowhere to be found. I walked to the kitchen, interrupting what she was doing.

"Chrissy!" I said, using a firm tone of voice.

"Oh, hey! I'm making you some burgers and fries," she said turning around, a bit startled.

"What's going on?"

"Nothing much, I just been working and—"

"You know what I mean! Why you put me in jail?" I demanded, cutting her off.

"I didn't put you in jail. You put yo'self in jail. I didn't press charges on you!" she shouted.

"Why would you report the car stolen? A car I bought!"

"Why would you be all up in some bitch face at a party?" she retorted sarcastically.

"Are you fuckin' serious?"

"Yes, I am serous!"

"You know what, I'll just go." I turned to leave. She ran up behind me and grabbed my arm.

"Nah. Bae, don't leave. I'm sorry!" she pleaded, sounding sincere.

"Don't leave? You're sorry? You know how much shit I just went through since you put me out and reported my car stolen?"

She wrapped her arms around me and pleaded continuously for me to stay, saying she was sorry. I've had other women in my life but she was my first love. So, as mad as I was, I couldn't help but forgive her. It felt so good to have her arms wrapped around me again. We stood there hugging until the smoke detector screamed. She rushed over to tend to the burnt food while I grabbed a towel and fanned the smoke away from the smoke detector. When Chrissy was finished with the kitchen, she walked over to the open window, where I stood laughing at the situation, and kissed me.

"Let's go in the room," she suggested, pulling me towards the bedroom. I followed behind her, staring at the jiggle of her butt in her pajama shorts.

In the bedroom we began kissing again. When I gripped her ass, she reached in the front of my pants and inside my boxers and started squeezing and stroking my joint. With it as hard as she wanted it, she snatched my bottoms down, pushing them to my ankles as she lowered herself until her lips were wrapped around my hardness. She began rolling her tongue round and around my tip while simultaneously bobbing it further and further in her mouth. I let her have her fun for a bit, then pulled her to her feet where we eagerly removed the rest of each other's clothes.

I cupped her ass in my hands, lifting her up, she wrapped her legs around me and began sucking on my bottom lip and neck. I laid her gently on the bed and climbed on top of her while kissing my way up the center of her body. At the same time as my lips reached her, my tip was parting her blossom. I eased it on inside of her wetness, smothering her sexy soft moans with my kiss. I pushed deeper and harder into her with every passionate stroke. Soon she was clawing at my back, that's when I pulled out and flipped her over. Instead of allowing me to keep control, she rolled from beneath me, pushed me down and took me in her mouth again for a hot second before climbing on top of me.

"I love you. I'm sorry. Tell me you ain't gonna leave?" she said in a soft moan while burying my full length deep in her warm box. "Please don't go."

With that said, I felt ready to explode, but I thought of the days I'd spent in the jail and quickly regrouped. I flipped her on all fours, and shoved her head in the pillows. The way she instantly arced her body turned me more on. I slammed my length in her and she pushed back. This was both of our favorite position. We both roughly pushed and pulled in and out until we came in unison.

"Bae, I love you," she said in a soft voice with her head resting on my chest.

"I love you too," I admitted, then my phone rang. "Hello?"

"Aye, Soldier, I gotta holla at you, bro!" Realla said, a little frantic.

"Wuddup?"

"Not right now. Tomorrow in person."

"Alright, fosho. Everything good though?"

"Might be, might not be. We gotta find a way to get to the bottom of it."

"Alright, I'ma hit yo' line in the morning then."

"Alright, mighty bro!"

"Love, my nigga!"

72

Chapter 12

I was in the best sleep I'd had in days, so when the familiar, annoying beeping of the alarm clock snatched me out of the sex-induced slumber, I fought to stay in it. Not long after the beeping started, it stopped, but then I felt Chrissy nudging me in the ribs.

"Bae! Wake up."

"Wuddup?" I grumbled, squinting over at the clock on the dresser. "Girl, it's five o'clock."

"You gotta take me to work."

"It's early as hell!"

"I'm working first shift today, so I gotta be there by six," she explained, as she rushed around the bedroom, getting herself together for work.

I rolled out of bed then dragged myself into the bathroom. After relieving my bladder, I brushed my teeth, washed my face, then put on the same clothes that I had on the day before, since I hadn't had time to shower.

"Bae, you gon' make me late. Hurry up!"

"Where my car keys?" I inquired while glancing back at the time. It was now 5:45 a.m.

"Here," she said, pulling them out of her drawer and handing them to me. "Now, let's go!"

We rushed out of the apartment to the car. I don't know if it was the thought of losing it or what, but it felt good to be behind the wheel of my whip again. I peeled out of the parking space and drove like 60 mph through the streets to her job. I made it there with a few minutes to spare. Chrissy kissed me goodbye, then rushed inside, and I headed back to the crib. Since I was out, I decided to see what was up with Realla—that's when the Boost Mobile automated phone operator let me know my phone was out of service. I would've panicked, but I had the money that Lil Wes and Maniac hit me with, so I made plans to go pay my bill after I showered and dressed.

As I passed Realla's grandmother's house, I spotted his car parked out front. I didn't want to knock on his grandmother's door because it was so early, and since I didn't have a way of calling his phone, I pulled up beside his car and set his car alarm off. I knew doing so would get his attention.

"Nigga, I was just trying to call you!" Realla exclaimed, poking his head outta an upper window to investigate what set the alarm off. "Hold on, I'm on my way down," he said after resetting the car alarm.

I turned on my hazard lights and sat double-parked, waiting on him to come out. He came strolling out about three minutes later and got in the car with me.

"What up, fool!" I greeted with a handshake.

"Man, it's some bullshit," he responded as I pulled off, heading on down to Chrissy's apartment.

"Some bullshit like what?"

"What you tell Lil Wes 'nem?"

"I ain't tell them niggas shit," I nonchalantly answered.

"Well, my auntie called me last night talkin' 'bout she know we broke in her crib and shit!"

"What! How she figure that?"

"Man, I don't know. At first, she said Maniac's name, and then she switched up and said her neighbors told her, talkin' 'bout they seen us and described our faces to her. I know that right there ain't true 'cause we were masked up, so it had to be them."

"Solid, man. I ain't tell 'em shit. They asked me what I got caught with, and I told 'em I got pinched with my heat and some weed. But I told them I took the weed from my mom's house 'cause somebody peeled me for my money while I was sleep. That's it. They don't know about the money I got knocked with or nothin'."

"Then them niggas had to tell her that hoe-ass shit!"

"Maybe she was just tryna catch you up in a lie. Maybe they ain't say nuthin'."

"See, there you go again, defending them busters! Stop givin' everybody the benefit of the doubt! You can't put shit past nobody!"

"Man, we been dealin' with them since we was kids. So what you sayin'? They ain't just some random-ass niggas!"

"Exactly! Now tell me, how long have they been fuckin' with each other before we started fuckin' with them?"

"It don't matter, lord!"

"It do matter! Not everybody loyal, my nigga."

We pulled up to the apartment building and went inside. I took a quick shower and got dressed while Realla sat in the living room waiting for me. When I walked out of the bedroom, Realla looked to be intensely texting on his phone.

"Aye, let's go to Boost so I can pay my phone bill, bro," I said, getting his attention.

On our way to Boost, we vented on our relationship issues with both our homies and our girls.

"What happened to them pills?" Realla asked, changing the subject. It wasn't until then that I remembered I had them.

"Oh shit!" I said, instantly pulling over.

"What?" Realla asked, nervously looking around.

"I forgot I put 'em in my spot right before I got pulled over." I dug into my secret stash past the cash and grabbed the sack of pills, holding them up for him to see.

"What you tryna do with 'em?"

"I don't know, maybe let muthafuckas on FB know I got Oxy on deck."

75

"Nah, don't do that. If you do, Maniac and Lil Wes gonna have evidence of us hittin' that crib," he stated as I pulled off into traffic again. "Soldier, you can defend them all you want, but I'm startin' not to trust 'em, on the real though."

"Anyway, what you think I should do with 'em then?"

"I don't care, as long as you don't talk to anybody that know them."

I took what he'd said into consideration and decided to holla at Aaron, the brother of this female I used to fuck on. I pulled up to the Boost Mobile store, and we both got out and went inside. Inside the store, I spotted Mack, the guy I'd met in county jail.

"Wuddup, bro?" I greeted, approaching Mack.

"Shit, what's good, fool?" he responded, looking genuinely happy to see me as we shook hands.

"You must've got out right after me or something?" I inquired.

"Yeah, like two hours after you left. What you 'bout to get on, though?"

"Shit, really, just coolin' with my nigga Realla," I said, pointing at Realla.

"Aye, I gotta show you something, bro," Mack whispered.

"Alright, let me pay my phone bill real quick." I paid my phone bill, then him, Realla, and some other guy that I assumed to be with Mack all walked outside.

"How y'all get here?" I asked Mack.

"We walked. This my lil brother," Mack said, introducing the other guy.

"Y'all can get in the car with us," I told him, then led the way to my car. Realla tapped my arm and gave me an angry look.

"Chill, I'ma drop 'em off real quick," I promised.

"Aye, this what I wanted to show you though, Soldier," Mack stated, reaching in his pocket and pulling out a wad of cash. I looked at the cash and then at him, waiting for him to explain, but all he did was smile. So I asked him why he was showing the money to me.

"It's counterfeit," he finally said, handing me one of the bills to examine.

"What you showing me for?" I asked, puzzled.

"'Cause, bro. I'm tryna sell some to put some real dollars in my pocket. I'm fucked up out here right now, I ain't gon' lie."

"I can't do nothing with no counterfeit money, Mack."

"What da fuck you mean, bro? Yes, we can! What you want for some of that?" Realla spoke up.

"$20 for a hundred," Mack said, and Realla immediately began peeling off $20 bills from his own bankroll. He handed Mack five $20 bills, and Mack gave him five $100 counterfeit bills.

"Now what you 'bout to do with that?" I asked Realla.

"I'ma finesse somebody outta something," Realla replied. What he said didn't sound too bad, so I got the same deal from Mack.

"Good lookin', y'all!" Mack said, putting the money in his pocket.

"Do y'all need me to drop y'all off somewhere?" I asked.

"Nah, I'ma go in this mu'fucka and pay my phone bill and try to sell some more of this."

"A'ight, cool. What yo' number?" I asked. Mack gave me his number. We all shook hands, and the two of them left. As I pulled off, me and Realla started discussing ways we could finesse people with the counterfeit.

"Bro, I know this nigga up on 60th and Villard who be selling *loud*. You could finesse him easy. He a lil nigga, like, eighteen years old," Realla suggested.

"Do he be holdin' though?"

"Yeah, he be having a lil roll on 'im."

"You got his number? Call 'im," I exclaimed, in a rush to see how it worked out for us.

"Nawl, I ain't got his number, but even if I did I couldn't call him 'cause he'll know that I had something to do with him getting finessed."

"How I'ma get him then?"

"He be out there posted at the gas station or in front of the lil corner store across the street."

"Alright, we'll roll up there later. Let's give him some time to make some money. I need some gas right now," I said, looking at my gas hand, wondering who Chrissy had driving my car.

"Let's go get something to eat, fool!" Realla said, rubbing his stomach.

I was feeling hungry as well, so we went to Wendy's. We sat in the car in the parking lot eating, laughing and talking about a lot of things we've been through together.

"Aye, let me see if this nigga can do somethin' with these pills," I said, pulling out my phone and calling Aaron.

"Wuddup, Soldier?" he sang playfully when he answered.

"Wuddup, bro! What you on?"

"Shit at the crib fuckin' with sis nem. You should see how her face lit up when I said yo' name," he said, laughing.

"Tell her I said wuddup. Aye, do you still know people who fuck with pills?"

"I know a lot of people who fuck with them. Why? You got some or you need some?" he asked.

"I got like ten of Oxis."

"What color?"

"They like light blue."

"Aw, them 20s."

"Can you get 'em off? I'll cut you in."

"Yeah, I got you. How you wanna do it?"

"I'ma bring 'em to you, off every dub you can keep five."

"Okay, cool. Is you coming through right now?"

"Yeah, I'm on my way." I hung up the phone and headed towards Aaron's.

"You a ole nice ass nigga!" Realla scolded me.

"What you talking 'bout this time?"

"Man, dude could play you in so many ways."

"Man, he ain't even like that. You don't know him."

"You right, I'ma leave it alone."

"Yo' fool ass!" I said, playfully nudging Realla.

Chapter 13

Okay, so after I dropped off 20 pills instead of the 10 pills I'd told Aaron about, I figured enough time had passed for our finesse target to have made some money, so I headed over to Villard Avenue. I could see that Realla was feeling some kinda way about me giving Aaron the pills like I did, but I needed to show him that he was wrong about Aaron. Truth be told, I was praying that Realla wasn't right at the same time.

When we pulled up to the location, it was busy as hell out there. People were roaming around, and cars were moving non-stop. I understood why a hustler would want to post up out there. Realla spotted the guy we were looking for making a sale in front of this bodega called the Ritz, located in a little shopping plaza right across from the gas station.

"I'ma throw my hood on and play sleep so he won't see my face," Realla schemed, thinking it would be the best way for him to have my back and not be seen.

"A'ight, cool!" I agreed, then pulled up in front of the Ritz and lowered my window. "Aye! You got some gas, bro?"

"Yeah, I'm good," he responded, strolling towards my window. I motioned for him to get in the back seat.

"What you was tryna get?" he asked, pulling out his bundle of weed.

"Just a twenty. Do you got change for a hundred, or should I run in the store real quick and get some?" I asked, hoping he said he had change.

"Nawl, I got it. You good."

We made the exchange, and he gave me four $20 bills.

"Alright then, good lookin', bro!" I thanked him, giving him a handshake. He got out of the car, and I pulled off. As soon as the car was in motion, Realla tossed his hood off his head with a big grin on his face.

"I told you he sweet!" he exclaimed, and we laughed about what we had just done as if it were the funniest thing in the world.

"Now, who you 'bout to finesse?" I asked.

"I don't know. I'm thinkin' 'bout going big and finessing somebody out some weight on some wurk. You know my guy on the South Side that we sold that merch to?"

"Yeah."

"Dude be hustlin' off these phones and be wanting muthafuckas to give them to work for 'im. He pay niggas off the pack they move. But I'm thinkin' if I bring my own merch without him knowin', I can get off his shit and mine, and make a quick come-up right quick," Realla explained, smiling about his master plan.

"That sound like a good idea. But do you know who you gonna finesse outta the wurk?"

"Yeah, I got somebody in mind."

That's all he said on it, so I left it alone. We rode around looking for other corner boys to finesse with the counterfeit money while smoking the free loud. I suggested we buy more counterfeit money, and buy a car with it, and then sell the car. We laughed and schemed until my phone rang. I looked at the screen and saw that it was Chrissy calling.

"Hello?"

"Bae, come get me from work. I'm sick," she whined.

"What happened?"

"I don't know, but before we left the house, I felt a little queasy. I thought it'd pass, but it got worse. I just got done throwing up."

"A'ight, here I come," I promised before ending the call.

"What's going on?" Realla inquired, relighting the last of the blunt.

"Chrissy said she's sick. She wants me to come get her."

"Aw, shit, drop me off."

"Why you say it like that?" I asked, heading in the direction of his grandmother's house.

"Shit, it sounds like she pregnant."

"Naw, dawg, that ain't it."

"Man, it's still morning and she sick. She pregnant, my nigga."

I heard what he was saying but didn't take it into consideration. Then thought, *What if she was pregnant?* I dropped Realla off at his grandma's house, then shot down to Chrissy's job. She was waiting out front for me when I pulled up. I helped her into the car, then headed home. Once inside the apartment, we discussed the possibilities of how she got sick, but Chrissy was the one who suggested, just to be on the safe side, that I should go to Walmart and get a pregnancy test. Right then, I thought maybe Realla knew what he was talking about after all.

I got nervous at the thought of having a kid. I knew having one meant I would have to be a lot more responsible. On my way to the store, I thought more about having a kid. Like, what if we have a boy? I would have to be a role model and teach him so much. Or what if we have a girl? I knew I would be super overprotective of her. I smiled at the thoughts as I pulled into the parking lot of Walmart and looked for a place to park. It was pretty packed to be so early. I found a slot between a white Pontiac Grand Prix and a silver Lexus. I looked at the female driver seated in the car next to me. She looked familiar to me, but I needed a better look to be sure if she was someone I knew or just a pretty face. We got out at about the same time, and that's when I recognized who she was. It was Lil Wes's girl, Keke.

"Wuddup, crumb!" I said jokingly.

"What up, littler crumb!" she retorted, laughing as she looked at me. Me and her didn't know each other extremely well, but we joked around with each other whenever we crossed paths.

"I see you riding nice. Who car you steal?"

"Nun uh, nigga, don't do me. This all me. I leave that car-stealing to y'all!" she exclaimed, chuckling.

"I'm fuckin' with you. Lil Wes told me you blessed him. That was some real shit you did lookin' out for him."

"What you talkin' about?"

"Lil Wes said you gave him a few gees and shit," I explained.

"Naw, if he told you that, his ass was just tryna hide that he gave me some money and bought me this car. And we're about to move in together soon. He told me y'all hit big but not to be talkin' about it to nobody, so that's probably why he said that." She shook her head, then said, "Don't tell him I said nothin'. I don't need him mad at me, even though I know y'all do everything together and shit."

"Damn, on what?" was all I could think to say in my surprise.

"Yeah, why? Wuddup?"

"Shit, I got you. I ain't know y'all was moving in together," I said, thinking fast. I couldn't believe that just maybe Lil Wes and Maniac had played me and Realla out of the money we hit that last lick for. "I gotta go in here and get this pregnancy test," I said, changing the subject.

"Aw, who pregnant?" Keke asked, sounding excited.

"My girl think she is," I answered, walking towards the entrance of the store.

"Lil Wes claim me and him gon' have a baby one day."

"That's wussup!" I said, still thinking about being played by my best friends.

Inside Walmart, we went our separate ways. I asked a lady with a Walmart vest on where the pregnancy tests were, and she led me to them. I sat there reading the boxes, then picked the one I felt was the best. With it, I went to the 10 items or less checkout line, which was very long. An older white woman rung up my purchase, and I paid her with one of the $20 bills that I'd finessed the young hustler out of. The cashier ran a marker across the bill, then popped the register open. She looked inside, then immediately closed it, informing me that she had to get change.

"How they don't got change for a twenty in the drawer?" I mumbled to myself, pulling out my phone and sending Chrissy a text letting her know I got the test and asking if she wanted anything to eat while I was out. While waiting on her reply and the cashier, I stood there tapping my fingers on the counter until I heard:

"Sir?" I turned and found myself staring into the faces of two police officers with the cashier standing behind them. "Sir, I'm going to need you to come with us, please," the bigger of the two officers told me.

"Go with you for what? What's the problem?" I demanded in response while complying with the officer's request.

"We'll tell you in a minute," the second officer said, walking closely behind me as I followed the big guy. They walked me to the exit, where they placed me in handcuffs.

"What the hell did I do?" I demanded, outraged.

"Possession of counterfeit money."

"I ain't had no counterfeit money, man!" I shouted, genuinely baffled. I instantly began thinking of a lie because I knew they were going to find the counterfeit $100 bills that I had on me.

"Well, that's not what the cashier is saying. She says you tried to buy a pregnancy test with a fake $20 bill," the big officer told me.

"Man, that's some bullshit!" I said as they placed me in the back of the squad car parked right outside the entrance of the busy store. Both officers got in the car, with the smaller, older one in the driver's seat.

"Well, tell us, how did you get it in your possession?" he asked.

"I found five hundred dollars outside my girl apartment building just now before I came to the store. I used some of it to buy the pregnancy test," I explained, hoping to sound convincing and praying that they believe me.

"Well, isn't that some trippy shit? You thought it was your lucky day and got played," the driver said, laughing.

"Yeah, we're going to have to check the rest of those bills," the big officer said.

We pulled into the garage of the police station and parked. The driver helped me out of the car and patted me down a second time. He took my cell phone, my car keys, and my money, counterfeit and real, and passed it to his partner.

"You got a lot of money here. I hope this all ain't no counterfeit, or you going down for a long time," the big cop informed me.

"Man, I told you, I ain't know it was counterfeit!" I shouted in defense.

With that said, they walked me out of the garage and inside the actual station, where I was cuffed to a bench. Then, right on the counter in front of me, they checked all the cash they'd taken off me and separated the real from the fake.

"Dude, you have $480 worth of counterfeit money. You wanna tell me what that's all about, or are you sticking to your story?" the big guy questioned.

"Man, I told y'all! I found five $100 bills outside my girl's apartment, and I used it to buy—or at least try to buy—the pregnancy test for my girl, and that's when y'all came and arrested me."

"So, basically, you're saying that you found five fake hundred-dollar bills?" he repeated.

"That's what it looks like to me," I responded nonchalantly.

"This story is getting more and more trippy."

"Yeah, the DA and judge should get a kick out of this shit," the other officer stated. A half hour later, they tossed me into a dirty, cold cell, and a few hours after that, I was off to the Milwaukee County jail for the second time.

Chapter 14

I woke up the next morning feeling extreme exasperation for being back in the county jail. Just to rub it in, I happened to be placed on the same pod that I was on my first time through. I didn't bother getting up for breakfast; I just laid there with my head buried beneath the hard wool blanket, wondering how long I would be sitting in jail this time. As soon as I noticed that my cellmate had gone out to the dayroom, I jumped out of bed and rushed to the phone. I called Chrissy. The automated operator explained that my call was being put through for a one-time complimentary call. When Chrissy answered, I instantly got excited.

"Hello?"

"Quan? Oh my God! What happened, Daquan?"

"It's a long story, Bae, but listen, I need you to come get the car keys from property and get the car from Walmart parking lot before it's towed."

"Okay, but tell me why the hell is you back in jail. You was supposed to be getting a pregnancy test and coming right back!" she fussed.

Before I could answer, the complimentary call had ended. I felt bad that the call wasn't longer, but also a little better knowing that she knew where I was and would be going to get my car. With nothing else to do, I went and sat in the TV area. I couldn't tell you what I was watching because I was in deep thought about my predicament.

"Say, cellie? You might wanna go in there and make yo' bed up if you tryna stay out here."

The sudden interruption snapped me out of my head. I looked over my shoulder and saw that the suggestion came from a guy that was here in the pod when I was there the first time. In fact, we went to court on the same day.

"Aw, wuddup, man! Yo' name Baker, right?"

"Yeah, just call me Assa," he said, taking a seat.

"Fosho. I'm Soldier," I introduced myself before going to make my bed. After I got it all made up, I laid right in it. I was kinda embarrassed to be around anyone that knew I'd just left. I couldn't do nothing but chuckle, thinking about my situation. How the hell did I get finessed by the person that I was finessing? While I was lying there thinking about the way Chrissy had welcomed me home when I got out the first time, Assa entered the cell.

"So, lil bro, what you doing back in the County?" he asked, then sat on his bed. I gave him the complete rundown of everything that went down from the time I got released all the way until I ended up in the cell with him.

"Ha, ha, ha, ha, ha!" he busted out laughing. "I don't mean to laugh at you, but that's fucked up!"

"Yeah, I'm already knowing," I said, laughing with him.

"What was you in here for the first time when we went to court?" he inquired. I told him about how I got caught up with a gun and some weed. I didn't forget to vent about how they took all my money for the second time.

"What did they do for you at court?"

"They just gave me another court date. My lawyer got me out on a PR bond."

Assa told me what he was locked up for, and as soon as he did, I remembered hearing about it on the news. When I told him that, he cleared up the lies being told by the media and people on social media. Learning a little about his life, for some odd reason, made me feel comfortable enough with him to give him the rundown of my past. I also shared stories with him about the experiences I've had since I'd been running the streets with my best friends. While I was running my mouth, he just sat nodding and shaking his head.

"Lil bro, to be real with you, I think you need to leave them so-called friends you got alone. Tighten up yo' circle, shit, focus on taking care of yo' family if yo' girl is pregnant. I don't know yo' life, but to me, them two niggas don't sound like they're real friends. It sounds more like they just using you for their personal benefit," he sincerely stated.

"Yeah, but I don't just wanna cut 'em off like that 'cause they the only friends I've ever had."

"Then you ain't never had no friends," he said, sounding like Mr. Marshal. "Always bet on self 'cause you all you got. Remember that. No matter how much somebody try to tell you different, ain't nobody gonna be fair with you like you are with them. What's important to you ain't important to nobody else. That's just how the streets are. Nothing is hardly ever mutual. Somebody will always love or even hate more than the other person that they feel those feelings towards. I didn't have anyone to tell me this; I learned the hard way. And from what you told me, you're going down the same bumpy road. But we got time to talk more in a minute. I gotta go make a call right quick," he said, then left the cell.

Alone again, I replayed everything that Assa had said about the ones I called friends. It was hard to believe, but what he said made a lot of sense. I really wanted to believe that me and my friends were all we got, like we tell each other. I really did, but it was getting harder to, especially knowing that they had played me and Realla out of our cut of the take from the robbery. I unknowingly slipped into dreamland but was awakened a few hours later by Assa informing me that it was count time.

Reluctantly, I dropped down off the top bunk and went to stand outside of the cell door. I saw the swampers preparing to hand out the food trays after the officer was done with his headcount. I watched the officer go from person to person, checking names and wristbands. When he was satisfied, he released the top tier to get their trays and then the bottom. Luckily for me, the meal being served was hotdogs, baked beans, and cookies, because I was starving.

Looking around, I spotted a few familiar faces from my last stay there, but nobody I knew personally. I finished eating, dumped my tray, and headed back to the cell. But before I could get there, the officer called my name and informed me that I had a professional visit. I promptly went out to the floor station, where an officer escorted me to a room where my public defender was waiting on me. I entered, closing the door behind me, and sat down.

"Mr. Walker, what happened?" he asked, looking up from his papers.

"Man, it's stupid, but I didn't intentionally commit a crime," I firmly stated.

"Yeah, yeah, that's what it looks like in the police report. We just have to get the DA to see it that way."

"What do you think gonna happen?" I anxiously inquired.

"It's hard to say at this point. There's not enough evidence to say you knowingly possessed counterfeit money. If the DA sees it that way, I can almost guarantee that it'll be dismissed." Hearing him say that made me instantly excited. I asked him when he thought I would be out. "Well, as of now, you have a pending bail-jumping case. But as long as the possession of counterfeit money gets thrown out, I'll see that you get back out on the original PR bond ASAP."

"Okay, cool!" I responded, doing my best to contain my excitement. When I got back in the pod, I found my cellie and told him what the lawyer had said.

"You should have yo' wristband checked to see if you've been charged. If the case been no processed, you good," Assa advised me.

"How I do that?"

"Just go up to the desk and ask the CO to scan yo' wristband for you." With that said, I started to go do as instructed, but Assa stopped me and said, "Not yet. If it was no processed already, your lawyer would've told you right then. So check yo' band after 7 o'clock when the computer update."

A bit disappointed, I sat back down in the TV area. Assa asked me what was I going to do differently when I got out.

"What you mean?"

"I mean, like if yo' girl pregnant, what you gonna do? Even if she ain't pregnant, what's yo' plan?"

"I can't even lie; I don't even know. I know I don't wanna work no punk-ass temp service job."

"Do you know how to hustle fo'real?"

"I know how to rob muthafuckas fo'real," I replied.

"You gotta get yo'self a real hustle," he retorted, grinning and shaking his head.

"What's the difference between robbing and hustling?"

"Don't get me wrong, it's all a hustle. Robbing is just not your hustle. It's what yo' guys put on you for their benefit. Anyway, it's a much less dangerous lane to get paid in. Anything can happen in the midst of a robbery, not saying shit can't go wrong in the middle of a drug deal, but it's rare. And flipping wurk, you'll appreciate yo' money more 'cause you kinda working for it as opposed to taking it."

"So you think I should pick up a pack?"

"I think you should get one of them punk-ass jobs and leave the streets alone, but since you made it clear that's not what you on, yeah. But not that shit yo' guy—what's his name—on. It feels better when you get it up yo'self." We sat there for hours talking about hustling. Assa told me how to serve, stack, re-up, and repeat. He also explained the game from the dopefiends' point of view, stressing to me how it's important to treat them like regular people instead of trash. The officer yelled, "Dayroom closed!" and everybody started heading to their cell.

"Why we gotta lock in?" I asked, getting up and following Assa to the cell.

"It's shift change," he answered, pointing to the clock on the wall above the officer's station. When we got in the cell, I jumped in my bunk.

"You might as well stay woke; we right back out in like fifteen minutes or so."

I sat up and continued our conversation about hustling. The more me and him talked, the more I liked him. He taught me a lot and seemed like he was too smart to be in his situation.

"Aye, Assa, man, you cool as hell. Give me yo' info before I leave."

"Man, for what? You ain't gon' write me."

"Yes, I am! Man, I'm for real," I stated sincerely.

"Everybody always promise to write people when they get out. But it never happens. But you know what? I'ma try you 'cause you seem like a real lil nigga."

"Man, when I say I'ma do something, I do it."

"Alright, well, check this out: since you good at robbing people, I could use yo' profession to help me and you out."

"What you need me to do?" I asked, eager to help my new friend.

"It's this nigga P. Nut off the East that owes me fifteen racks for some wurk I fronted him. Now the nigga call himself not paying 'cause I'm locked up. I want you to go get that from him, and just send me eight so I'll be straight for a minute when I get up North."

"Dude be holdin'?"

"The nigga be having money. He move a little weight, but he a bitch! He ain't never really been in no real shit, so if you put that heat in his face, he gonna tell you where his mama's stash at."

"So how you think I should do it?"

"He stupid; he be goin' around jackin' with like 20 to 30 gees on him. I wouldn't send you off. Lil bro, he sweet. I need you to make sure he knows I sent you at him, though."

"I got you." After I wrote everything down, I gave Assa my number and my mother's address.

Chapter 15

Fuck what the Feds saw
I don't agree with the law
I got pounds and keys in the wall
Dope and weed in my drawers
I ain't worried 'bout beef
Got hands and heats like Steven Seagal
I be droppin' these niggas like leaves in the fall
An' I got scratch like fleas on a dog
I be goin' hard like, Kareem with a ball
An' I don't show no love,
Charlie Sheen these broads
I be dressed in all black, like Batman
They tryna stop me from eatin' like Pac-man
I'm tryna get my weight up, like a fat man
I'm familiar with these streets like the back hand
Never trust a bitch, and tell her where the stash spot
She fuck with them jack boys, on the last block
Never trust a muthafucka on the crack pot
I'm dedicated to the game, like a mascot . . .

Standing outside of my cell door, waiting on the second shift officer to finish barking out his expectations for the evening, I decided to try to use the phone again. When the officer finished giving his speech and opened the dayroom, I raced to the phone tree closest to me. When I reached for one of the four phones, some guy tried to take it out of my hand. I held it, and he scowled, waiting for me to let go.

"This Folks' phone, fam!" he stated as if that meant something to me.

"Man, miss me with that shit. I'm using the phone," I replied, standing my ground as I snatched the phone receiver out of his hand and began dialing my number.

"Bitch-ass nigga, you got me fucked up!" dude yelled, then tried to snatch the phone back.

I shoved him with my free hand, immediately dropping the receiver and getting in my fighting stance, prepared for him to come at me. Before he recovered, a few guys nearby intervened.

"Y'all niggas gonna get the damn dayroom shut down, y'all trippin'!" one of the guys exclaimed.

"Yeah, y'all take that shit in one of them cells if that's what y'all really tryna do," another one that I'd seen kicking it with Assa said.

"Say nomo. When I'm done with the phone, we thumpin', fuck-boy!" I said, picking the receiver up and dialing Realla's number. I put my back to the phone to keep my eye on the punk as I waited for Realla to answer.

"Hello?" he said, accepting the complimentary call.

"Wuddup, bro, I need you to go tell Chrissy I just talked to my lawyer and I should be getting right back out," I said, rushing, knowing our time was limited.

"Soldier, what the hell you do?"

"Long story, my nigga. This call gonna hang up. But tell her to come get my keys and go get my car ASAP."

"A'ight," Realla replied right as the call ended.

I hung up the phone, then scanned the dayroom for Mr. Phone Check so I could work off some of my frustration. I spotted him at a table with a couple of his guys talking not far from where Assa and his guys were seated. I walked over to their table and asked the punk if he was ready to throw hands.

"Aye, sit down one time, my guy, let us holla at you," one of the guys at the table with him said.

"I'll holla at y'all when we done thumpin'."

"That's what we tryna holla at you about. We tryna deaden this shit."

"Nah, I'm good. Dude called me a bitch. We either going in the cell or I'm takin' off on him right here!"

The two guys looked at each other, then at the dude I was challenging to a fight.

"So what you gon' do?" Assa asked the guy I wanted to fight.

"It's whatever to me, O.G.," he answered, staring me down.

"Let's go then, hoe-ass nigga!" I barked, leading the way to my cell. Inside the cell, I walked straight to the back and faced the door, waiting for my opponent to enter.

Since we aren't allowed anything but cheap thong shower shoes in the county jail, to avoid slipping and sliding, I took off my shower shoes and socks. A few moments later, dude entered the cell. I noticed that he had on his shower shoes with his socks tied around his ankles, holding up his pant legs. He left the door slightly cracked open behind him so it wouldn't lock us inside. Then he foolishly tried removing his shirt. As soon as his arm went up, I hit him with two quick, hard jabs in the face. He immediately abandoned his idea, his shirt falling back over his head as he swung blindly back at me. One of his wild fists brushed my chin, unfading me, but stung enough that I knew to dodge the second one. I swung a hard combination of rights and lefts, only landing two before he grabbed me in a tight bear hug. We started tussling. He slammed me into everything in the small cell. I slipped my right arm free and viciously slammed my fist into the side of his face and head. He tried shielding his face by burying it into my chest. Doing this made him loosen his grip, allowing me to get my left arm free. I grabbed a hold of his afro with both hands and headbutted him in the mouth. Blood instantly started pouring from his mouth.

He pushed me away, simultaneously grabbing a fistful of my dreads and pulling. I dipped down, grabbed his legs, scooping him off his feet, and slammed him to the floor. He held on to my hair, so we both went down. That didn't stop me from slamming my fists full force into his face. He let go of my hair to block the punishment. One of my blows slipped through his guard, dazing him. That's when I really let loose. I stood up and started stomping him, kicking him. Mad about him pulling out some of my hair, I jumped down on his torso with both feet.

"A'ight, I'm done! I'm done!" he shouted in surrender.

"Get yo' bitch ass out my cell!" While he was getting up to leave, I punched him in the back of the head. He stumbled and ran out of the cell.

I quickly cleaned up the blood from the wall and floor, then looked in the mirror to see if I had any noticeable bruises or scratches. He'd only hit me one good time, so I was good. I put my socks and shower shoes back on, then went into the dayroom.

"Y'all didn't mess the cell up, did y'all?" Assa asked when I dropped down in the seat next to him.

"Nawl, I got it together, it's still good." I sat there with him and his guys, listening to them tell old war stories until it was time for dinner. It was some kinda slop for dinner, so I just ate bread and drank the juice. I had a killer headache from the fight, so I went right in the cell and laid down. I was in bed for maybe five minutes before I fell off to sleep.

I woke up because I had to piss. When I hopped down off my bed, I was surprised to find Assa asleep. That made me wonder how late it was. I looked out the cell door window at the clock and saw it was after four in the morning. I whispered aloud to myself, "Damn, I been asleep for a minute." I relieved myself, washed my hands, and hopped back on my bed. I couldn't fall right back to sleep, so I lay there thinking about my life and everything. I wasn't a drug dealer, but Assa made some good points about it that was better than the way I'd been living. Right then, I figured I may as well give it a try. While I was thinking of all of the ways I was going to ball outta control, I fell back asleep.

"Aye, Soldier, get up. She doing wristband checks," Assa said, nudging me.

I got out of bed and stood at the door. When Officer McCoy checked my wristband, I went back in the cell, brushed my teeth, and washed my face. When I was done, I lined back up outside the door just as McCoy was announcing who had court. Then she called the tiers individually to get our breakfast trays. I grabbed my tray and sat next to Assa and his guys in the TV area.

"Them two must've came in last night," I heard Assa's guy say after I took a bite out of the biscuit on my tray.

I looked up, looked around, and asked who he was referring to. He pointed at two guys sitting at the table right behind us.

When I looked where he'd pointed, I couldn't believe my eyes. One of them was the young dude Realla put me on to finesse with the counterfeit money.

"Assa, that's dude right there," I whispered excitedly.

"Who?"

"The dude I tried to finesse with the counterfeit." He began laughing and asked me what I was going to get on with him. "I'ma act like he played me, and if he say something about what I gave him, I'ma act like I don't know," I answered, smiling.

"So what, you gon' whoop his ass too?" Assa's homeboy asked, chuckling.

"I'm thinking about it." The three of us burst out laughing. I finished eating my food and dumped my tray.

I walked over to the dude that I tried to finesse with the counterfeit money. "Aye, let me holla at you, fam," I said,

98

tapping his shoulder. To my surprise, he got up and followed me away from the others.

"You know them twenties you gave me was fake, right?"

"What you talking about?" he asked, looking puzzled.

"I bought some gas from you over in the plaza on Villard, and you gave me four fake $20 bills," I explained to refresh his memory. "I'm in this bitch 'cause I got caught trying to spend one of 'em. That's how I know they were fake."

"Man, that shit must be floating around 'cause somebody got me too," he said with a straight face.

"That ain't got nothing to do with me though," I snapped.

"I'm saying I ain't know I had no fake dubs on me. Shit, I just got caught tryna spend a counterfeit hundred that I ain't know I had."

"Man, you gotta give me my bread back. I ain't taking no loss like that," I said, getting a little loud and upset like I didn't play him the same way.

"Man, if you don't get yo' broke ass out my face!" he barked, then walked away from me. Before I could react, my cellmate came walking up, asking me not to get loud anymore because the officer was watching.

"I'm about to run in his room and scrap him."

"Don't get yo' lil ass caught in there," Assa cautioned me.

After breakfast, Officer McCoy gave her expectations, then opened the dayroom as usual. The dude I wanted to fight went and got on the phone, so I sat at a table near the TV area where I could watch the entire area. I was waiting for ole boy to head in his cell so I could follow behind him. I watched his every move. He walked around and talked briefly to a few guys, then he tried getting on the phone a few more times before finally going in his cell. When I got to his door, he was pulling it closed. I caught it and invited myself in.

His back was turned, so he didn't notice me come in. I shoved him in the back, sending him sailing to the back of the cell and crashing onto the concrete slab used as a desk.

Before he could regroup, I started raining heavy fists. I landed at least four before he covered his face with his arms. Thinking about the fight I had the day before, I snatched his legs from under him before he got a chance to grab me. As he went down, he hit his head on the desk.

At this point, he was more focused on the pain coming from the back of his head than me. I took advantage and stood over him, raining punches down on his head and face. I don't know if it was intentional or not, but he kicked me in the nuts. I immediately ran out of his cell as fast as I could. I walked slightly hunched over from the pain that was shooting through me from his kick. I made it to my cell; I didn't even bother getting on my bunk—I just dropped right on Assa's bed, rocking back and forth holding my groin.

"So, you got yo' ass whooped, huh?" Assa inquired, coming in the cell, laughing at me lying there rocking in pain.

"Man, naw, his bitch ass kicked me in the nuts."

"God don't like a bully. Is you gonna be alright?" he asked.

"I better, or I'm killing his bitch ass when I catch him again!"

Assa left the cell, and I lay there for a few more minutes until the pain went away. I got up and returned to the dayroom. The guy I'd just fought with was nowhere in sight, so I decided to have my wristband checked since I forgot to do it when Assa told me to. As the officer scanned my booking number to check the computer, I had butterflies in my stomach. When she told me that my possession of counterfeit money charge had been no processed, I almost jumped with excitement. I rushed to the TV area and told Assa right away.

"You should be getting released soon then. Don't quote me on that, but you should be," he said after I told him the news.

100

I sat in the dayroom talking to Assa and his homeboy and watching my back from the dudes I fought.

"Anthony and Parker?" the officer yelled from behind the desk. I looked up at the officer's desk and stood up. "Pack up, y'all getting released," she informed us.

I shook Assa and his homeboys' hands, then I went to the room and stripped my bed, collecting everything they gave me when I came in. I stuck the paper with the information Assa gave me in my sock. Before I walked out the room, Assa walked in.

"Don't forget about me, man," Assa said.

"I got you, man, I promise," I replied, shaking his hand again.

We talked until the doors popped for dayroom.

Chapter 16

I emerged from the hell of the County jail for a second time. Staring at my cell phone, I became overwhelmed with thoughts, unsure of who to call. I reflected on the conversations I had with Assa, so I didn't wanna call my so-called friends. And Chrissy never came and picked up my keys like I asked her to, nor did she put money on her phone to talk to me once she became aware that I was locked up. That made me question her feelings for me, but not much. There was the possibility that she was pregnant. While briskly putting some distance between me and the jail, I thought of schemes to take control of my life for once. All of my plans involved me investing in someone new. That's when I thought of Loni, the girl from the Eastside party. I scrolled through my contacts to see if I still had her number. I did. I pressed *send*, and the phone started ringing. I was thinking of what to say when suddenly the ringing stopped.

"Hello?" she sounded sexy as hell.

"Hey, wussup, it's Soldier," I casually reintroduced myself.

"Who?"

"Soldier! I met you at that party on the Eastside. I was the dark skin dude with the dreads and all the tattoos."

"Aw, okay, I know who you are now. Hey, wussup! Why you just now calling me?"

"It's a long story, but do you think you can do me a favor if you not busy?"

"So you take forever to call me, and when you do, you ask for a favor. I'm curious, so sure, wuddup?"

"Do you have a car or have access to one?"

"Yeah, I can use my mother's car."

"Okay, cool. I just got outta the County, and I need you to come get me."

"Okay, give me like five minutes and I'll be on my way."

"Okay, thanks! I'll be walking up Highland." I hung up the phone, and Fetty Wap's song—*Trap Queen*—popped into my mind. I began thinking of ways I could use her to my advantage because it was time for me to get on my grown man. About 10 minutes and 15 blocks later, my phone rang.

"Hello?" I answered, seeing it was her.

"What street you on now?" she asked.

"I'm on 25th and Highland. Where you at?"

"Okay, I see you." A few moments later, a white Nissan Murano stopped beside me. I looked inside and saw it was Loni driving, and I got in the front seat.

"Dang, you musty!" she said, smiling and covering her nose as she pulled off.

"Well, hi to you too," I retorted but couldn't help but laugh.

"What was you in the County jail for?"

"I had bought some weed from some nigga, and he slipped me some counterfeit money that I got caught with." I left out the part about me trying to put one over on him first. I didn't want to give her the impression that I was shiesty.

"So what they do? Just made you sit in jail?"

"Pretty much. They decided not to charge me. Well, they couldn't charge me because I didn't know I had the fake money."

"Oh, what made you call me?"

"I just been going through a lot, and I needed a change. So I figured I'd take this time to get to know you."

"So where am I taking you?"

"Oh, my bad. I gotta go get my car out of Walmart parking lot on East Capitol."

"Why were you walking up numbers and not towards Walmart?"

"Ha, ha, ha, I don't even know!"

Loni turned the car around and headed towards Walmart. On the way there, we didn't talk much. I pretty much just listened to her rap along to Nicki Minaj as she drove. I kept the information I shared to a minimum. I didn't want her knowing too much about me so soon. When we got to Walmart, I directed her to my car. I was happy to see that it was still there, especially since I had a gee in the stash. The jail released me $25 cash and a check for the rest of the real money that I had on me when I got locked up.

"Here you go," she stated flatly, stopping next to my car.

"Aye, I want to kick it with you, but I ain't tryna be smelling like this or wearing these clothes. Can you go in there and grab me something to change into?" I asked, seeing if she was willing to contribute her services any further.

"Sure, what do you want me to get?"

"Just some sweats, a shirt, some socks, and some underwear so I can shower at your place."

"So you got it all planned out, huh?" she said, smiling, holding her hand out as she stared at me.

"What?" I asked, smiling back.

"Where the money?"

"Man, you buy it," I said, playfully pushing her hand away.

"How you know if I got some money?"

"Because pretty girls keep money."

"Well, how you know if I wanna spend my money on you?"

"It's a short-term loan. Now, are you going to get the stuff or not, dude?"

"I can see that you gon' be a problem already," she scoffed. "And don't call me dude," she said before getting outta the car and going in the store.

While Loni was inside, I got in my car and got the money out of the stash, then got back in her car. Thinking of my plans, I decided not to call Realla yet and put him up on the move Assa asked me to do. I wanted to get a little more familiar with Loni. I sat there trying to decide how much about me I wanted her to know as I was planning my change. The car door opened, interrupting my thoughts.

"I got everything and you some deodorant because you ain't using mine," she giggled, placing the bag on my lap.

"Thank you. I'ma think about you when I get right," I joked as I moved to get the money to repay her.

"Don't worry about it. It didn't even cost much."

"Okay, then I'm about to get in my car and trail you to yo' crib."

"Okay."

It felt wonderful being behind the wheel again. I realized being incarcerated makes you start to appreciate the little things in life. It was a short ride to Loni's house since she lived on the Eastside. I followed her into an alley where she pulled inside a gate. I did the same. We both parked and got out, and I followed her to the back door, ogling her ass and surveying my surroundings. Inside, she led me up some stairs. The upper unit door was slightly ajar.

"Y'all always leave y'all door open like that?" I inquired, a little suspicious.

"Yeah, why not?"

"Don't you got neighbors?"

"My mom my neighbor."

"So you live upstairs from yo' mom?"

"Yeah, she owns this house."

I told myself that Ms. Loni was going to be real beneficial to my future, then immediately asked her to point me to the shower. She led me to the bathroom. From what I could see, her crib was a nice size; everything was neat and clean, and it had a fresh smell to it. After I showered and dressed, I bagged up my dirty clothes and threw them in the trash.

"Why did you throw your clothes away?" she inquired.

"I went to jail in that shit. That make it bad luck," I explained, and Loni rolled her eyes, giving me a cute smile. She was naturally pretty. "Let's sit down and talk," I suggested. She led me into the living room where we sat on a black leather couch.

"Ain't no jealous ass boyfriend gon' pop up on us, is it?"

"Nawl, he's working a double, so you good," she nonchalantly replied.

"Aw, man, I'm outta here!" I sprang to my feet.

"I'm just playing, sit down," she said, laughing hysterically.

"Aw, you a jokester?" I smiled, sitting down.

"Sometimes. I ain't gotta worry about no crazy babymama stalking you, do I?"

"That's kinda what I wanna talk to you about."

"Oh my Gwud!" she exclaimed. "It's always something with you niggas!"

"Man, chill, you assuming things without knowing the facts."

"Okay, well, let me hear the facts then."

"Damn, you sound like a crazy stalker babymama," I said, giving her a smile.

"Whatever!" She rolled her eyes.

"Okay, check it out. I was messing with this chick for a while that might be pregnant. The day I got locked up, I was tryna buy a pregnancy test. That's why my car was at Walmart. Me and her been going through some shit. We kinda broke up and this pregnancy shit is crazy."

"And that's where I come in at, huh?"

"Don't say it like you a rebound or something," I said, sensing she was getting upset.

"That's what it sounds like."

"Loni, I been through too much bullshit lately to be gettin' myself into some more bullshit. I'm not trying to get no money out of you, fuck on you and move around, or whatever else you think my intentions are. It just seems like I can't trust nobody, and I need somebody I can trust. Somebody that's gonna support my decisions, somebody who can turn a bad day into a good one, somebody who's willin' to help me get somewhere in life instead of holding me back. I just need a real friend. But, dude, if you feel like I'm on some bullshit, I'll leave right now."

"You don't gotta go."

"You sure? You ain't gonna get bipolar on me and change yo' mind, are you?"

"Keep calling me dude and I'ma change my mind."

"Is it cool if I stay the night? I don't want nobody to know I'm out yet, and I really wanna get to know you better."

"I wanna know you too." She got quiet for a moment, then asked, "You hungry?"

"Can you cook?" She laughed, then admitted that she's not a gourmet cook but she knew her way around the kitchen.

"It can't be worse than County food," I joked.

She got up and disappeared into the kitchen, leaving me in the living room. I grabbed the remote off the coffee table and turned the TV on. She had cable, so I turned it to ESPN.

"Bags, do you eat nachos?" Loni asked, walking back into the living room.

"What kinda person don't eat nachos?"

"You'd be surprised," she said, leaving again.

I sat there flipping through channels until she returned carrying a big platter of nachos and two cans of orange soda.

"Damn, girl, you decorated the shit outta this plate. You must've used to work at Taco Bell or something. I ain't gon' be able to eat all of this."

"This for the both of us, crazy," she explained, laughing as she sat down beside me. We ate and talked. I still kept

107

what I shared about myself to a minimum. Before we knew it, hours had passed.

"Dang, it got late quick," Loni announced.

"Yeah, it did."

"Thanks for being honest with me earlier."

"Thanks for still accepting me after knowing who I was. You real cool."

"Can I kiss you?" she asked with the same shyness that she gave me when I first met her. I answered her with a kiss. Before I could pull back, she wrapped her arms around me, deepening the kiss.

"Let's go in my room," Loni suggested, taking my hand and leading me into her bedroom.

Locked in a heated, lusty urgency, we wasted no time getting undressed. We removed each other's clothes while still kissing. She had me so ready that I was on the edge just from the warmth of her skin. She pulled away, laying on the bed invitingly, staring up at me. I climbed between her knees, kissing my way up her inner thigh past her mound. I briefly considered going in for a taste as I kissed my way to her lips. Completely on top of her, she let out a sexy moan as my tip parted her split and her body tensed like she hadn't been touched in a while. I eased further into her tightness, and she instantly came. She felt so good that I had to refrain from going nuts and pounding her out. Instead, I gave her long, deep strokes. With every one, she opened a little more. I gradually increased my force and speed, making her moan louder and louder. She had me so turned on that I had to pull out not to bust too quickly. When I did, she took control, pushing me down on the bed and taking my length in her mouth until it touched her throat. To be honest, she gave some of the best head that I'd ever had. I still wasn't ready for our fuck session to end, so before I gave her what she was sucking for, I pulled her off. She immediately climbed on top of me, guiding my hardness back inside of her. I gripped her waist and slapped her ass as she rocked and bounced. She rode me so good that this time I couldn't stop myself from busting. I released, buried inside her. After a few seconds of Loni aggressively grinding on me, I felt her legs clamp on my hips, and I knew she was climaxing. She soaked me, then collapsed on my chest with my length still inside her.

"That was fun," Loni confessed in a breathy giggle. "Bags, I'ma take you from yo' girl."

"That's highly possible!" I retorted. We both laughed and lay silently, holding each other until we fell asleep.

Chapter 17

I woke up that morning to an empty bed and the aroma of breakfast in the air. I rolled out of the bed naked and followed my nose to the kitchen. Like I knew she would be, Loni was standing at the stove cooking.

"Hey, beautiful?" I greeted. When Loni saw me, her eyes went wide. She immediately pushed me back out of the kitchen.

"Put some clothes on; my lil' sister here!"

"Oh, shit! My bad. Can I wash you off of me?"

"Fine, hurry up and get in the bathroom," she exclaimed, grinning while ogling my well-built body. She returned to the stove, and I grabbed my clothes and took a quick shower.

"What you cookin'?" I asked, entering the kitchen fully dressed this time.

"Cheesy jalapeño eggs, pancakes, and bacon."

"I hope you didn't do it just for me 'cause I don't eat pork."

"Well, good, we don't eat pork either. It's turkey bacon."

"You tryna take me from ole girl fo'real, huh?" We laughed, then she explained that she and her family are Muslim.

"Ahh, okay," was all I could think to say.

"Are you Islamic?"

"Nawl, I don't really believe there's a God."

"Nooo, why not?"

"That's another long story for another time," I said, then sat down at the table. "So, where's yo' lil' sister?"

"In her room, since some people don't believe in putting on clothes," she retorted, shaking her head. "Re-Re!" she yelled for her sister.

"My bad fo'real! I wasn't thinking," I apologized.

"It's okay. I wasn't either," she admitted just as a little girl, approximately eight years old, came running into the kitchen.

"Huh?" the little girl exclaimed, instantly freezing in place when she saw me.

"I want you to meet my friend. His name Soldier."

"Hi," Re-Re shyly greeted.

"Hey," I replied with a little friendly wave.

"You can go back in your room now," Loni excused her, and she took off back to her room.

"I take it that she stay up here with you?"

"Yeah, my mama has me look after her while she's working."

I heard my cellphone ringing and went to retrieve it from where I'd left it on the arm of the sofa. It was an unknown number calling. Curious, I answered it, and to my surprise, it was a prepaid call from Assa. I accepted the call right away.

"Wuddup!"

"Soldier Bags, wuss good?"

"Shit, man, just gettin' shit together like we discussed," I explained.

"That's wussup. I ain't finna keep you long. I just wanted to make sure this was your number since you didn't put a name on the paper."

"Aw, my bad."

"Lil' bro, try and take care of that as soon as you can. I just tried to call the bank, and the punk rejected my call."

"Say nomo, I'ma make the withdrawal and deposit like I said I would." Before Assa could respond, the battery died on my phone. *I hope he didn't think I had hung up on him*, I thought, as I walked back into the kitchen.

Loni handed me a plate with three pancakes, a pile of eggs, and a few strips of bacon on it.

"From the frown on yo' face, that must've been yo' girl calling, huh?"

"No, that was my guy in jail. He need me to do something for him, and my phone died in the middle of the call," I explained, then told her that I had to go.

"When are you coming back?"

"When do you want me back?"

"I don't want you to leave just yet, but you can come back whenever you want."

I couldn't believe how comfortable she was with me coming and going. I could see that Loni was serious about taking me from Chrissy. I finished eating, then gave her some goodbye kisses when she walked me to the door. I jumped in my car and immediately put my phone on the charger, then pulled out of the gate. As I drove off, Chrissy popped into my mind. I found myself comparing her to Loni.

I needed to talk to Realla about the move I'd promised to do for the big homie, but the closer I got to the apartment, I wasn't sure if I should scoop Realla up first or go see Christina. I decided to go see Chrissy. When I pulled up to the apartment building, a feeling of dread came over me. I don't know why, but it did. I headed inside and let myself in. Stepping through the door, I was hit with the odor of stale weed smoke. That made me wonder about her possibly being pregnant and how she would be as a mother. I found her naked, asleep in the bedroom. I walked over and kissed her awake.

"Umm," she purred, opening her eyes. "Shit! Daquan, when you get out?" she asked, springing upright, startled to see me and sounding more irritated than excited that I was there.

"I just got out," I answered, stepping away from the bed and looking around the messy room.

"You lying, Quan. I went to pick up your keys last night, and they said you got out that afternoon! So where you been?"

I wasn't prepared for this response. I had to think of a lie quick. I didn't want to say I was at my mom's crib just in case she already checked there. Instead of lying, I told her the truth.

"Man, ain't nobody lying to you! I got out yesterday, went and got my car, then just stayed out tryna clear my head."

"Whatever, nigga! If that's all you did, then why you didn't call me?"

"Why in the fuck didn't you call me?" I retorted. "See, dude, you be trippin' over silly shit!"

"Well, since I be trippin' so much, you can give me my keys and get out!"

"Wow! Why the fuck is you really doing this, Chrissy?" I asked, so exasperated with her that tears welled in my eyes. She didn't even try to answer me. She just twisted her lips and rolled her eyes, holding her hand out for the key. I shook my head and started taking the apartment key off the ring.

"Nawl, nigga, car keys too!"

"Chrissy, I paid for that car."

"But it's in my name! Let me get my keys, nigga, or do I gotta call the police?" she threatened. I tossed her the keys and walked away. She followed behind me, talking shit and shoving me, trying to provoke me into a fight.

"And just to let you know, bitch, I'm pregnant. So you need to go get a job or something to help take care of this baby."

"Just take my shit to my mama crib!" I shouted, walking out and slamming the door. As soon as I got out in the hallway, I called Realla.

"Soldier! What da fuck it do, boy?" he answered excitedly.

"Shit, bro, where you at?" I asked, sounding like my dog just died.

113

"I'm at my grams' crib. What's wrong with you?"

"I'll tell you when I get there. I'm on my way." I headed up the street to his grandmother's house. When I got there, I texted him to let him know I was outside. He let me in, and we went into his room.

"What's going on, my nigga?" he asked again.

"Man, Chrissy just put me out again! And the bitch took my car keys, screamin' that it's in her name and shit!"

"Damn, why she trippin' like that? You just got out?" he asked, just as confused as I was. I explained what she was tripping about.

"Damn, nigga, you caught! Shorty got her own crib and she bad?"

"Yeah, but I'm just tryna use the bitch for a duck-off and to come up. So don't tell nobody about her."

"I got you, my bro."

"Where yo' car at?"

"It's out back. Why, wuddup? Where you need to go?" I told him about the few days that I'd done in the County. We laughed about the fact that the dude I tried to finesse with the counterfeit got locked up for the same shit and my fight with him. Then I told him about the favor that I promised Assa I would take care of.

"You know I bought my car from Assa, right? He's cool as hell. So when you wanna handle that for him?"

"I don't know, but we gonna have to do some homework first, bro." I pulled out the paper with the information that I'd written down about our target. "Dude drive a Pepsi blue Volvo sittin' on some white and blue twenty-fos. He live on the East but be over on 28th and Atkinson. He stands about 6'1", light skin with braids. He be going to all of the clubs. Mainly, what we lookin' for is his car 'cause it stands out. If we find it, we find him."

"You know them boys on Atkinson get down, right?"

"Yeah, I know how they rockin', but like I said, he don't live over there. It's just where he hustle."

"It don't matter to me. I'm just lettin' you know that I'm not playin' with nobody that come at us."

Realla suggested that we ride through Atkinson and case the scene. I agreed and drove over there. Almost everywhere in that neighborhood, people were outside. We watched people standing on the bus stops get harassed by the young hoodlums. We circled through the blocks looking for the car. I wasn't surprised that it wasn't out there. It was still early, so he was probably still at home. Realla's phone started ringing, and he instantly pulled over and answered it. By the aggressive tone he was using, I knew it was his girl that he was talking to. They're always arguing, but no matter what, at the end of the day, they were best friends. That made me question my relationship with Chrissy even more.

With nothing to do, I pulled out my phone and opened the notepad, then began writing a rap about how I was feeling.

Hard times got me feelin' like fuck da world
And my side bitch got me feelin' like fuck my girl
I'm in da streets so I'm always on my P's and Q's
I chase paper like a real man 'pose to do
She's unhappy, I don't get it, I'm so confused
I love my bitch, I love money, how am I 'pose to choose
And to make things worse, now there a baby involved
If I scream move, bitches, she'll be takin' it all . . .

I was just getting in my flow when Realla suddenly interrupted me.

"Yo, yo, Soldier! You see that?" he pointed to a Volvo that fit the description.

"Yeah, I see it. Let's see what he look like when he get out." We waited with our eyes glued on the car. A light-skinned dude with a big Afro stepped out, carrying two McDonald's bags. After we saw which house he went in, Realla drove off.

"We got his ass!" I shouted in excitement.

"Let's get 'im right now."

"We ain't ready, bro."

"Come on now, Lord, we always ready," he said, handing me one of his trusty guns. I sat back and followed his lead, knowing he had a plan.

A text came through on my phone. It was Loni, and it read, "Hey, what you doing?" I texted back, "Can you say crazy, stalker babymama :-)." She replied, "LMAO! Whatever. I'm just asking b'cuz u rushed out like it was an emergency." I couldn't reply because Realla was ordering me out of the car.

"Come on, let's go," he exclaimed.

"Bro, you tryna run up in there with no masks?"

"Hell yeah!"

I asked Realla where we were, and he told me that we were parked behind a house across the street from our target. We casually walked across the street and onto our target's porch. Realla knocked on the door. Within moments, without asking who was there, the door was opened by the guy with the big Afro. Realla put his gun to his head, pushing him back in the house. I kicked the door shut and shot him in the face. Startled, I almost panicked but kept my focus. I pulled my shirt up halfway over my face, then moved further into the house. In the living room was an even lighter-skinned guy with braids and gold teeth sitting on the couch with his hands in the air, terrified. I trained my gun on him.

"Where the merch at?" I demanded as Realla took off to search the house.

"What merch?" the guy asked.

"Muthafucka, don't play crazy! Guns, drugs, money, where that shit at?"

"This all we got. We was just about to re-up," he pointed to the two large McDonald's bags on the table in front of him. I peeked inside one of the bags and saw it was filled with cash.

116

"I want what's in yo' pockets too, nigga! And by the way, Assa said you should've paid yo' debt." Before he could say anything, I shot him twice in the chest. Then I grabbed both bags of cash and went looking for Realla. He ran out of the room he was in, stuffing what looked like a kilo in his pants.

"Yo, let's go!" I yelled from the doorway.

We sprinted from the house in case someone heard the shots. We jumped in Realla's car and smashed off.

Chapter 18

Back inside Realla's bedroom, we dumped the bags of rubber-banded bundles of cash on the bed. Instead of counting one of the bundles of money to see how much had been banded together to make things a bit easier, we foolishly started unbinding the money. It took us at least a half hour to count and re-band the money. The ending total of the money from the bags was $90,000 on the dot—our biggest lick ever. I immediately counted out $20,000 and set it aside, then evenly split the remaining $70,000 between the two of us.

"What's that there for?" Realla inquired about the cash I'd set aside.

"This for Assa. I'ma put it on his books."

"Why you giving him so much?"

"I told you dude owed him. I gave him a lil extra for putting us up on it. Bro, he gonna need this shit to keep fighting to get out," I explained.

"Okay, yeah, you right."

"You ain't find nothing in the house?" I asked, thinking that he was planning on surprising me with his find like I was planning on doing with the cash I'd taken outta dude's pockets.

"Hell naw!"

"Really?" I said, a little more shocked than I meant to. I know I'd seen him stuff a large package in his pants. I instantly thought about how Lil Wes and Maniac had played

118

us out of the take from that last lick the three of us pulled together. I took a deep breath to check my emotions, thinking that maybe none of my friends were to be trusted like Assa had said. I decided not to mention the money that I'd taken off the guy's person.

"Oh yeah, I found this shit," he said, pulling some jewelry out of his pocket. It wasn't the pocket I seen him stuff the dope in, so I know there wasn't a misunderstanding. I bet he stashed what I'd seen him with when he went to the bathroom before we got to counting the money.

"This it?" I asked, digging through the jewelry he tossed on the bed.

"Hell yeah."

My feelings were so hurt knowing Realla was lying to me. I just knew that it was "we're all we got" with me and him, but I see not. Having all that money in front of me made it a little easier to drop the issue, but I told myself I'd never forget it. Looking through the jewelry, a gold and silver diamond tennis bracelet caught my eye. I checked it thoroughly, trying to see if it was real, and I saw *24k* engraved on it. Believe it or not, my first thought was to give it to Chrissy, but then I remembered her punk ass just put me out and took my car. So I decided to use it to thank Loni.

"Aye, I'ma keep this, fool," I announced, holding up the bracelet.

"Go ahead. You can keep all that shit."

"Naw, I'm straight with this here." I stuffed it in my pocket. "I gotta buy me a car," I said aloud.

"Man, you better go get yo' shit from Chrissy."

"Nah, I'ma get something I can put in my name. I'm tired of going through bullshit with her."

"I know somebody selling something," Realla said, grabbing his phone.

"What they got?"

"A Chrysler Sebring, and he only want two gees for it."

"Man, I don't want no muthafuckin' Sebring!" I exclaimed, laughing.

"Just buy it until you find something you want. Then you can sell it."

I thought about what he suggested. I did need a car right away.

"You right, fuck it, call him."

Realla called up the guy selling the car and told him he had a buyer. The guy agreed to meet us for the sale, so I collected all of my money, put it in one of the bags, then followed Realla out to his car. I couldn't believe I had over $35,000 that I didn't have to split. I also couldn't believe that we had killed two people for it. I had no intention on killing anyone. My plan was to pistol-whip the guy, maybe shoot him in the leg as a message from the big homie. But when Realla killed the first guy for no reason, it made the other guy believe he was next, so he tried to fight for his life. I don't blame him—I would've done the same thing.

I wondered what Realla was feeling about the situation because he didn't seem fazed by it at all. His demeanor kinda had me wondering would he go around bragging about it. To be safe, I decided to get rid of the gun. Soon, Realla pulled into a Walgreens parking lot located on 35th and Wisconsin Avenue.

"See, that's the car over there," Realla pointed, then parked his car beside a 4-door maroon Chrysler Sebring. We got out and met with a tall, elderly Black guy.

"Hey, wussup, Realla!" the man greeted, shaking Realla's hand.

"This my guy who wants to buy the car," Realla said, pointing to me.

"Man, it's a runner. Do you wanna test drive it?" the seller offered, talking to me.

"Naw, I'm cool. I'm not gonna keep it long anyway. I just need something to get around in for the moment."

"Okay, well, if you care to know, I fixed the brakes and new taillights. Other than that, it's in good condition."

"Okay, cool, you want two gees for it, right?" I confirmed before sitting back in Realla's car and counting out the money. I took it from the wad of cash that I didn't split with Realla. I got back out and handed the seller the money, and he gave me the keys, a bill of sale, and signed the title over to me. We shook hands, then he got in the passenger seat of a brand new Cadillac DTS.

"Realla, how do you be knowing these muthafuckas?" I asked, collecting my bag off his car seat.

"That's my granddad's mechanic—or was—before my granddad passed. He did the work on my car."

"Well, good lookin' on this, bro. I'm about to go put this money on big homie's books and buy me something to wear."

"Alright, my nigga, I'll holla at you," Realla replied, and we went our separate ways.

The real reason I wanted to get away from him is because I couldn't stop thinking of Realla's betrayal, and I was anxious to get rid of the gun. I drove straight down to the Milwaukee River and dropped the gun over the bridge with a sigh of relief. I got back in the car and headed to the County jail and put $20,000 on Assa's books. On the way there, I received a call from Loni and remembered that I'd never answered her last text.

"Hello?"

"Why you ain't text me back?"

"My bad, I had got busy for a minute. Wuddup though?" I talked to Loni until I got to the cashier's window at the jail. The cashier gave me a hard time about the money, but in the end, she put $19,500 on his account, taking a tip for herself.

With that taken care of, I drove to Playmakers on 3rd and North Avenue to buy me something to change into. I left the bag of money beneath the driver's seat in the car and went in the store with the rest of the money that I didn't split with

Realla. I bought a couple of outfits with shoes to match and left. I changed clothes in the car right in the parking lot, stuffing everything that I took off in the Playmakers bag and throwing it in the dumpster. I didn't have anything else to do, so I called Loni back.

"Heeey, bae!"

"What you doing?"

"Nothing, sitting here watching *The Jungle Book* for the hundredth time with Re-Re," she answered, and I heard her little sister laughing in the background.

"Y'all wanna go get some ice cream or something?"

"Yes, get me outta this house, please!" she said, being dramatic. Re-Re yelled that she wanted to get out of the house too, and I couldn't help but laugh at her cuteness. "Give us a few minutes to get ready."

I agreed, and we got off the phone. I passed the time by going to the gas station and filling up the gas tank. There, I bought a sack of weed from some guy getting gas beside me. I made sure to air the car out before I pulled up to the back of Loni's house. This time, I stuffed the bag of money inside the dashboard. I knew that I needed to find a safer place to put it, but that did the trick for the time being. All set, I texted Loni that I was outside, and shortly after, the two sisters were exiting the house. Re-Re suggested that we go to Dairy Queen, so off we went. Once there, we ordered a bunch of different flavors of ice cream and had our own little tasting party. Re-Re was enjoying herself, mixing scoops of each flavor. Seeing the little girl pigging out like that made both of us laugh.

"So, what you do when you left?" Loni questioned.

"Dang, girl, you nosey!" I said, laughing. She didn't respond; she just rolled her eyes and smiled.

"My nigga called from the County, and I had to go take care of some stuff for him," I repeated what I'd told her before I left that morning.

"Whose car is that we in?"

"Mine. I just bought it until I find me something new."

"What happened to your other car?"

"It's in ole girl's name, and she got on some punk shit and took it from me."

"I thought it was yours."

"I did too. I paid for it. But I put it in her name, so . . . well." I explained, shaking my head.

"Yeah, right! So you just let her take it?"

I admitted to her that I'd gone to see Chrissy and how she had flipped out on me and threatened to call the police if I didn't give her the keys. I also told her about the time she'd done it before.

"Oops, I ain't mean to get you in trouble," she said, smiling. I couldn't help but smile, knowing what she was thinking.

"So where are you going to stay since she put you out?"

"I got enough money to live good out here."

"Where? On the streets?"

"Yup!"

"So you just gon' live on the streets?" she asked again in disbelief.

"Yeah, I'ma be a homeless ass baller." We both burst into laughter.

"You can stay with me."

"It ain't too soon?"

"Not to me. We already done . . . you know," she said, pausing and smiling. We both looked at her lil sister, but she wasn't paying attention to us—she was too occupied with the ice cream.

"Okay, cool. Aw, yeah, before I forget." I pulled out the bracelet and handed it to Loni.

"What's this for?"

"Remember when I told you I was gonna think about you when I got right?"

"I told you not to worry about it," she said, smiling.

123

"Man, whatever. Let me see that." I grabbed the bracelet and put it on her wrist.

"Oh my God! It is so cute, thank you!" she said, rotating her wrist and checking it out.

"You deserve it."

We finished stuffing our faces with ice cream and went back to her house. When we got there, I felt a little tired, so I climbed in Loni's bed and took a nap.

"Soldier!" I heard Loni yelling and nudging me in the back. "Yo' phone keep ringing," she said, slightly irritated.

"Okay, I'm up," I grumbled, opening my eyes. I got up, and she rolled over and went back to sleep. Looking at my phone, I was surprised to see it was Chrissy calling. Before I answered, I noticed the time was 8:43 p.m.

"Hello?" I answered, going in the bathroom to pee.

"What took you so long to answer?"

"I was asleep," I responded, annoyed.

"Where you at?"

"What do you want?"

"You to come home," she said in a soft voice.

"What? No!" I raised my voice to let her know I was serious.

"Why not?"

"Bitch, think about it! I'll see you when I see you." I hung up and powered off the phone. I was always a pushover when it came to her. It felt good being able to do what I did. Maybe she'll think about it before she put me out again.

"Loni?" I said, grabbing her and shaking her to wake her up. "I'm hungry."

"Well, go make you something to eat."

"I want you to do it."

"Why?" she complained.

"I can't cook."

"Babe, I'm sleepy."

"Man, never mind. I'm going back to sleep." I stripped down to my boxers and got under the covers. Grabbing Loni by the waist, I pulled her closer, and she snuggled in. I lay there with my arm wrapped around her soft, warm body, loving the way she felt.

Chapter 19

"Al hamdu lil lahi rabbil 'alamin. Arrahmanir rahim. Maliki yawmiddin. Iyyaka na'budu wa iyyaka nasta'in. Ihdinas siratal mustaqim. Siratal ladhina an'amta'alaihim, ghairil maghdubi'alaihim wa lad dhallin. (Amin)"

The harmonious sound of Loni's Islamic prayer pulled me out of the grasp of the gruesome dream of the murder I'd committed. Opening my eyes, I saw Loni prostrated in a corner of her bedroom, dressed from head to foot in a beautiful white and gold prayer gown. I sat up in bed, watching and listening to her for a moment, then felt like I was somehow invading her privacy, so I grabbed my phone, put on my pants, and tiptoed into the bathroom. When I powered on the phone, instantly a bunch of text messages and missed call notifications appeared on the screen. It was super early in the morning, so I put off reading the messages until I got up for the day. I finished up in the bathroom and returned to the bedroom to find Loni sitting at the foot of the bed in only her bra and panties.

"Are you about to leave?" she asked, sounding a little disappointed.

"No, why?"

"Just asking. Do you want me to make you breakfast since the baby was so hungry last night?" she teased, giving me that smile of hers.

"Hmm, how about I have you for breakfast?" I replied, briskly closing the space between us. Before she could get her words out, I dropped to my knees, scooped her legs up in my hands, tossing one leg over my shoulder in one fluent motion. She let out a little squeal that turned into moans when she felt my warm breath in her middle, and my tongue parted her lips. Using only my tongue, I tickled her sweet clit. She almost lasted a full round until I sucked it into my mouth. Instantly, her soft thigh closed around my head, and her body started bucking against my mouth as she came. I pried myself away, laughing at her.

"A-a-ain't nothing funny!" she fussed in a breathless voice.

"I told you I was hungry," I joked as I stood and pushed my full hard 8½ inches inside her. I ain't gonna lie, I bust in less than three minutes. "Fuuuck, girl!" I growled, pulling out and releasing on her belly. Now she was laughing at me.

"Do you want me to cook or not?" she asked on her way out of the bedroom.

"Let's go to the mall. We can get somethin' to eat there."

"Okay, but I'ma have to give Re-Re some cereal or she's gonna be cranky. What mall do you wanna go to?"

"I ain't been to Bay Shore in a while. Let's start there. I heard they put in some new stores," I answered, sitting on the bed and counting the remaining cash that I had in my pocket. Assa was right about that guy—after buying the car and the two outfits, I still had over $6,000 that I'd taken off him.

"Good. I already know where I wanna eat," she yelled from the bathroom.

A little while later, I heard the shower running, so I checked the text messages and missed calls on my phone. All but one of the text messages were from Chrissy cussin' me out, talking about I'm cheating on her. Sounding like her punk ass didn't rob me and put me out. At that point in my life, I was tired of being gullible and passive. The time I spent conversing with the big homie in the County had me looking at life completely different. The odd text was from Realla inquiring about my wellbeing. I also had a few missed calls from him and an unknown number. When I looked up from my phone, Loni and Re-Re were standing in the bedroom doorway, dressed and ready to go.

"Y'all lookin' cute," I complimented them.

"Thank you!" Re-Re said in her shy voice.

"Come on, let's go," Loni said, pulling my hand. I got up, and we headed out of the door. On the drive to the mall, Realla called.

"Aye, Lord, wuddit do, fool!" he exclaimed when I answered.

"Shit, wussup?"

"Man, I thought yo' ass went back to jail."

"Nawl, I'm good, bro bro. I'm chillin' with shortie I told you about."

"Oh yeah? What y'all 'bout to do?"

"We on our way to the mall right now."

"Okay, okay, hit me when you leave."

"I got you, fool." I hung up the phone and pulled into the mall's parking structure, taking the first slot available. The first place we went was to the Cheesecake Factory to eat.

"I need a whole new wardrobe," I blurted out when we were exiting the restaurant.

"Why?" Loni asked.

"Because I don't want to go get my clothes from where I used to stay, and I'ma need a change of clothes every day if I'ma be staying with you, right?"

"Right," Loni agreed, smiling about me moving in with her.

"Y'all can grab whatever y'all want too."

"You sure? 'Cause that's the wrong thing to tell me."

"Yeah, let's go crazy."

"Babe, where you get all this money from all of a sudden?"

"Somebody owed me some money for a favor I did."

"That must've been a serious favor," she said, sounding skeptical.

"Don't worry about it," I said, playfully bumping into her.

We wandered the mall from store to store. In no time, all three of us were hauling multiple bags of clothes and stuff. The sudden ringing of my phone pulled me away from Loni's kiss. I saw it was the unknown caller again. Answering, I learned it was a prepaid call from Assa. I quickly accepted, happy to hear from him.

"Wuddup, big homie!"

"Wuss good with you?"

"Shit, out and about with my new lady friend, doing a lil shopping."

"That's wussup. I see you were true to yo' word. I got that slip and was like, damn! That was good looking, lil bro, straight up! Damn, you move fast."

"Ha-ha, hell yeah. I told you I had you though."

"Aye, I got something else for you for handling that for me."

"What is it?"

"You'll see. Call this number on three-way for me." He gave me the number; I called, and a woman picked up. I clicked him back in, and he ordered her to give me the title and keys to his Mercedes. I almost exploded with excitement.

"Lil bro, where you at right now?" Assa asked.

"I'm at Bay Shore."

"Bay Shore Mall?"

"Yeah."

"That's a convenient coincidence," he said, then told me where to go to pick up the car and everything.

I informed Loni that we had to go pick up the car, and we left. When I saw the Mercedes parked in the storage space, I got even more excited. The car was factory silver with cream interior, not a scratch anyplace on it. I climbed behind the wheel, feeling like I was dreaming as I drove back to Loni's with her and Re-Re following me in the Chrysler.

"He really just let you have this car?" Loni asked once we were in her driveway.

"Yeah, this mine now."

"So what are you gonna do with this one?"

"I don't know, maybe sell it," I answered, helping her grab all our bags out of the Chrysler. We took them in the house, then I ran back out to the Chrysler and pulled the bag of money from the stash in the dashboard. After I'd counted it up at Realla's the day I got it, I bundled it in $5,000 stacks to make it easier to count. So now I took two of the bundles and put the rest back in the dash, then went back in the house.

"Loni, would you put my stuff up for me? I gotta go handle something right quick."

"No, you don't—you about to go see yo' babymama."

"What? Huh?"

"I'm just playing. I got it," Loni said, laughing. I walked up behind her and put my arms around her while she was hanging the clothes in the closet.

"You don't gotta worry about her."

"I'm not. I was just playing." She spun around and kissed me.

"Here, you can hold on to these in case y'all wanna get back outta the house." I gave her back the keys to the Chrysler, then went and got in the new whip and smashed off. The real reason I had to leave was to show Realla the car. I immediately pulled out my phone and dialed his number.

"Yo!" Realla answered the phone.

"Where you at, fool?"

"In traffic. Where you at?"

"I just got out here. You tryna meet up?"

"Hell yeah. Meet me in Midtown. I'm already comin' down Fond du Lac."

"I'm on my way." I hung up, cranked the radio, and put some pressure on the accelerator to see what luxury power feels like. I felt like a boss with my pockets loaded with cash and driving a luxury vehicle that was all mine. I felt that I needed some jewelry to add to my image. There was a jewelry store in the Midtown shopping center, so that's where I went and purchased a $2,500 gold watch with crushed diamonds on its face, a $2,800 gold moneybag pendant, and a small box link chain. Because I'd spent all that money in the store, they gave me some square-shaped diamond earrings. Now really feeling myself, I texted Realla and asked him where he was. He said he was at the gas station, and I told him that I was pulling up on him.

I crossed over to the gas station, parked helter-skelter in front of him, got out, and turned my swag all the way up.

"Damn, my nigga, you lookin' like new money!" Realla said, stepping from the pump to get a better view of me and my ride.

"I feel like it too, my nigga!" I excitedly replied.

"How much you cash on the Benz?"

"Nothing, it was a gift from Assa," I answered proudly.

"Get the fuck outta here!" Realla exclaimed, a bit skeptical.

"No bullshit."

"Man, you copped this with that twenty geez, didn't you?"

"Realla, get off that bullshit. On the nickel, I put that shit on his books," I said, offended by his accusation. How he gonna accuse me of being cut-throat when he's the one cuffing merch? I wanted to get at him about that but decided to let it go.

"If it was anybody else, Soldier, I wouldn't believe it, but you a stand-up dude, so . . . damn."

"You know I wouldn't do that shit to you, bro bro."

"Yeah, my nigga, I trust you. So what we doing?"

"I don't know. What you tryna do?" I asked, not really feeling like being around him after he'd just accused me of

131

cheating him out of that money. One of the things that Assa told me is, if someone doesn't trust you when you haven't given them a reason not to, then most likely they not to be trusted. Assa had dropped a lot of jewels on me that opened my eyes to a lot.

"I know some bitches on the South Side we can go kick it with," Realla suggested.

"Naw, I ain't tryna go south bound."

"Well, what you tryna do?"

"Realla, fo' fo'real, I'm tryna blow some more of this cash and boss my life up. You with me?"

"Indeed!" he agreed, and we jumped in our cars and pulled off. With Realla tailing me, I zipped down to Eastside Auto Body & Customs to see what they offered.

"Don't tell me you about to get that clean muthafucka painted?" Realla asked, staring at my car.

"I told you once I found my car what I was doin' to it."

"What color you doing it?"

"I ain't sure, but I'ma do it *outrageous*, whatever I choose," I retorted, entering the building. One of the employees actually remembered the car from Assa bringing it in for a price quote. It was hard for me to choose a color, so I went with my favorite—Ruby Red. I also told them to lift it and fit it for 26-inch rims, but another shop employee convinced me that 24-inch rims would give it a look, so I went with that. I put a $5,000 down payment on the job and handed over the keys.

"Man, I feel like you tryna flex on me," he said, smiling.

"Ya know I might be!" I retorted, rotating my wrist so my watch could flicker on him in the sunlight. Before he could hit me with a snappy comeback, his phone rang.

"Aye, bro, shortie want me to come home," he said, sounding disappointed.

"Is it cool if I post up at y'all crib with you and have shortie come scoop me?"

"Yeah, my bitch in a good mood today. You know when a nigga money funny, hoes be actin' sour. But when yo' shit right, they be sweet as honey."

"Yeah, we should nickname 'em Sour Patch Kids." We burst out laughing. I pulled out my phone and texted Loni, asking her to come get me and giving her the address. By the time we pulled up to his house, Loni was texting, saying that she was almost there.

"You tryna burn one before shortie get here?" Realla asked. I said yeah, so the two of us sat on the porch, smoking a blunt until Loni arrived to take me home.

Chapter 20

Loni had done some redecorating while I was gone. Her bedroom was now set up to include me. One of the first things I noticed was that she'd added another hanging shoe shelf with my shoes displayed on it to the wall in the area that was originally her prayer corner. Seeing this kinda made me feel bad because I enjoyed being awakened by her harmonic prayer. That simple act showed me that she was serious about building on our relationship.

"Babe, did you eat while you were out?" she asked, walking past the bedroom.

"No, what's on the menu though?"

"Re-Re wants gyros. Do you eat that, or should I make you something else?"

"Gyros are good. They'll be extra fire if you got some cucumber sauce to go with 'em."

"I make my own," she proudly stated.

While the girls were in the kitchen preparing the meal, I set up the Xbox game system that I picked up that day and connected it to the TV in the living room. I was just getting the hang of the new Madden game when Loni entered the room with my food and a tall glass of Kool-Aid.

"Do you always eat in here?"

"No, I usually eat in the dining room with my sister."

"Then let's do that. I don't want you changing up everything 'cause I'm here, and I don't want Miss Re-Re mad at me for taking you away from her," I said, getting up and following her into the dining room where her sister was already eating.

"So what's wrong with the car?" Loni asked, then bit into her gyro.

"Nothin'. I put it in the shop to get it personalized so it'll really feel like mine."

"My mom loves this bracelet. I think she a lil jealous," she said, giggling. The three of us sat talking until we were done eating, then Re-Re went into her bedroom to finish playing with the toys she picked up at the mall earlier, leaving me and Loni to clean up.

After helping her with the dishes, I challenged her to a game, but she declined, saying it wasn't fair because she don't know how to play it. But she sat beside me while I played. For the first time, I noticed her posting on social media. I didn't think she was into it, because unlike Chrissy, who was always on it in everybody's business and putting everyone in hers, Loni seemed to just be reading and watching video posts. Soon she excused herself and went in her room to get herself ready for prayer. This time her lil sister joined her. Not wanting to be disrespectful, I turned off the game and went into the bedroom and read some of the stuff that Chrissy had posted on social media. I couldn't believe that she was trying to play the victim, making me out to be the bad guy who left her when she got pregnant. To be a jerk, I posted a pic of my iced-out watch and wrote: *Only time will tell,* then I hit "like" on all of her negative posts about me and logged off.

Loni returned, and we discussed her religion, which explained why she did things the way she does. Somewhere in our conversing, we found time for kissing that turned into us fucking ourselves unconscious. I rolled over and found myself once again alone in bed, only this time it wasn't the sound of her praying that I heard, but her having a conversation with someone. I got up to go to the bathroom as well as to be nosey. When I walked in the kitchen, I saw where Loni got her good looks from. The woman that I instantly knew was Loni's and Re-Re's mother was approximately 5'8", with perfect curves and a buttermilk complexion. She looked at me when I entered the room, with the same hazel-like colored eyes as her oldest daughter.

"Mama, this is my boyfriend that I was telling you about," Loni introduced me.

"You didn't tell me he was here," she scolded her, then extended her hand to me. "Hi, how you doing?"

"I'm well, and yourself?" I replied, shaking her hand, glad that I was fully dressed.

"My daughters were just telling me that you took them on a mini shopping spree. You wouldn't happen to be a drug dealer, would you?"

"Not that I know of," I said with a nervous chuckle.

"Then what do you do for a living?"

"I do private security and repo work." I didn't really lie—just used fancier words to describe how I made my money.

"Okay. My name is Bianca, but you can call me Mom if you like. Lady tells me that you call yourself Soldier Bags. What's that about?"

"Oh, so Miss Re-Re wasn't misspeaking when she called you Lady," I said teasingly to Loni, smiling. "I don't call myself that. My mother and older brother gave me the name because 'Bag' was my first word, and those little green toy soldiers were my best friends when I was little," I explained, giving Loni's mom a smile.

"That's cute," Bianca smiled. "What's your birth name?"

"Daquan, but everybody call me Quan."

"Well, it was nice to meet you, Soldier. Lady, we'll finish talking later," she said, then left out of the backdoor. I waited until I could no longer hear her on the stairs before I said another word.

"Why you tell her that I'm your boyfriend?"

"What was I supposed to tell her? That you're some dude I'm laying up with? I promise you, she would've killed us both."

"She would've killed you. I know how to get outta Dodge."

"Whatever! You need to stop 'cause you know you're going to be my man anyway. You already are; you just don't wanna admit it," she explained, giving me a devious smile.

"I'll admit it when you show me all of you. I know you gotta Sour Patch Kid somewhere in you."

"A what?"

"Never mind. Aye, I need you to hold something down for me."

"What is it?"

"It's just some money. I need you to hold onto it just in case something happens, and so I don't blow it all."

"Okay, I got you. Even though I know you just tryna test me. You ain't slick."

"I'm not testing you, Lady Pooh. I'm serious."

"Ah, don't call me that!" she said, chasing me around the table, trying to hit me. I ran out to the Chrysler, retrieved the money, and came back in the house. I gave Loni $10,000 to put up for me, keeping $15,000 to work with.

"Don't tell nobody you got this."

"I won't. I swear," she promised, then placed the money inside a shoebox and buried it in the back of the closet.

"Aye, Loni, you know you my bitch, right?"

"Yeah, but you need to see that I can be so much more. If you let me in, I'll be everything that you told me you needed in your life and more. Leave all that foul shit with that crazy chick like you left all of your old stuff with her."

Before she said anything, I hadn't looked at me leaving my stuff with Chrissy as me getting away from my past. I just didn't want to deal with her or give her any reason to put me back in jail. Sitting on the bed, watching Loni get ready for the day, I thought of how much better my life is already with her. Everything about the beauty in front of me was better than the one I had. Honestly, the only thing that Chrissy had on Loni was the years that we'd known each other and the child that she's possibly carrying. I wasn't doubting if the baby was mine; I was doubting the pregnancy itself. I needed proof.

Chapter 21

Man, dude, I don't mean to drag my sob story out, but what else do I gotta do but sit dying slow in a cell? Keep it real—yo' nosey ass wanna be all up in my business anyway. So when you look at it, we're doing each other a favor. Okay, okay, to move along, I'ma skip through all of the mushy-mushy shit I did with Loni within that next couple of weeks after meeting her fine-ass mother. Would you believe that the big homie Assa knows Loni's mother? Yeah, I don't know if that was fate or coincidence. All I know is that after he spoke to her on the phone, she seemed way more comfortable with me being around. Okay, right quick, this is how I found out that they knew each other, and then I'ma start wrapping this shit up because this is day 89, and if the DA don't come with it soon, I'm outta this bitch. I'll explain all of that soon. But anyways . . .

Loni walked in the room and saw me in deep thought. I could feel her staring at me, so I asked her, "Wussup?"

"I'm just wondering what are you doing on that phone that got you concentrating so hard," she answered, plopping down beside me on the loveseat.

"I'm not concentratin' hard on nothin'. This here is effortless to me!" I boasted, showing her the lyrics I'd written on my phone. "I write raps and stuff to help me think better. If that makes any sense to you?"

"Yeah, I get it. It's like when I recite the Al-Faatihah when I'm irritated."

"Now I know what you be mumbling under yo' breath when you mad at me."

"I don't be mad. I know that you just do shit to irritate me on purpose, just to see what I'ma do. Ahh, I don't wanna hear no excuses. I do wanna hear what you wrote though. Pleeease?"

"I got you, but it's still a work in progress," I forewarned her, then cleared my throat and recited what I'd written to her:

When I touch down I'ma need a package of hard
And I'ma hustle 'til I'm dead or 'til I'm back in the yard
Cause I done seen how it feel to be reliant on fam
And to be honest, boy, I rather just rely on the yam
So y'all could act nonexistent and keep y'all distance
And don't be insistin' on giving assistance
I ain't trustin' no bitches; the love ain't consistent
They'll ride or die for you up 'til you get sentenced
If it's one thing I regret, it's being raised in a church
I spent way too much time believin' prayer would work
Actions speak louder than words—should've considered that first
Time to get my hands dirty, and I don't play in dirt
Fuck the Feds, I won't talk unless I'm pleading the fifth
I don't do codefendants; they don't stick to the script
When the plug make the call, then I'm taking a trip
And don't be thinkin' I'ma lick 'cause I'ma shoot from the hip.

"That's it so far. I don't even know what I'ma call it."

"Babe, can I ask you something?"

"Yeah, go 'head." I put down the phone so she knew she had my attention.

"Do you really regret being raised in church?"

"I wasn't really raised in church. My foster parents were church folks. My foster mom was a mean bitch that cheated on her husband and hated me because I didn't fuck her. An' I used to sometimes go to Sunday School when I lived with my real mother. Honestly, I never really took it serious. I went there to eat and to get away from all of the bullshit in my home. So when I said that I spent too much time believin' prayer would work, I meant it. I prayed and prayed when I was little, and bad shit kept happening to me. So I stopped praying and started makin' shit happen for myself."

"That's sad," Loni said, with tears falling. "I'm sorry that you went through that."

"Don't cry, it's okay. That was a long time ago. If I'd known you was gonna get to actin' like a girl, I wouldn't have let you hear it," I said with a chuckle, half joking with her.

"I am a girl, you ass!" she retorted, wrapping her arms around me and resting her head on my chest.

"Well, that's fucked up. All this time I thought I was fuckin' with a woman," I teased, holding her tight so she wouldn't slug me for my comment. My plan for not getting hurt didn't work out for me because she bit my nipple. We started playfully tussling, and Re-Re suddenly appeared outta nowhere, joining in and helping her big sister chase me through the house. All of the commotion that the three of us were making brought their mother upstairs to investigate. I could tell by the look on their mother's face that she thought we were really fighting. It didn't help that when she entered the living room, I had Loni pinned on the floor with Re-Re tugging at my arm trying to free her. The only thing that saved me was that we were laughing.

"If you three don't stop all that ruckus, I'ma start kickin' some tail for real!"

"They started it," I ratted, letting Loni up.

"Snitches get stitches, Soldier!" Re-Re threatened, waving her little fist. We burst out laughing.

"Re, where you learn that from?" her mother inquired as she began re-twisting one of Re-Re's pigtails that had gotten frizzy in our play. While Re-Re explained the cartoon that she'd learned the phrase from, my phone rang, saving me from any further scolding.

"Wuss good, Assa!" I answered excitedly.

"Assa? Soldier, did you say Asa or Assa?"

"Who dat asking about me?" he immediately asked after overhearing Loni's mother inquire.

"That's my girl's mother. Hold on right quick though," I told him, then turned to her and told her that I'd said Assa.

"Oh my gawd! Let me talk to him."

"Assa, she wanna holla at you, bro." He agreed, and I handed her the phone. I stared at Loni with questioning eyes, and she hunched her shoulders, not having a clue. We both stood there eavesdropping on their conversation.

"Assa, these kids all up in my mouth. Take down my number and call me as soon as you hang up with him," she gave him her info, then passed me back the phone.

"Hello?"

"Lil Lord, I've been knowing Bianca ass for years. The last time I seen her was at Club 502 where my mom bartends. If Bianca's daughter is anything like her mother, you caught. Don't mess that up."

"Yeah, the only difference is Loni a lil darker than her mother. But anyway, wuddup? I know you called for a reason."

"Damn, I can't just be checkin' in with my lil guy?"

"I ain't sayin' that. I just thought you had some news about what happen at court, that's all."

"So you ain't heard, huh?"

"Nawl, wuddup?"

"They didn't give me First Degree Intentional because they seen that it was self-defense, which means I'm no longer facing life. But it's not over because they felt I used too much force to stop the threat, so they hit me with Second Degree Intentional."

"That's good. How much they tryna hit you with now?"

"I don't know. Everybody I talk to thinks I'ma get like 5 in and 5 out, but I don't know. Anyway, how you livin'? Say, lil bro, Killa Rob says wuddup and stay outta bullshit," he said, relaying a message from his guy that he was always with in the County.

"Tell 'im wuddup, and I'm on a whole 'nother level now. Big bro, I hope you get back out here 'cause I'm tryna level up. I ain't tryna go backwards."

"Shit, you don't gotta wait fo' me to do that. Just hit up 2Blacc. How much time do we got left on this call?" No sooner than the question left his lips, the operator informed us that we had a minute left on the call. "Aye, I'ma call right back, and I want you to call him."

"Okay." The phone went dead, then about two minutes later it rang again.

"What it do?" Assa gave me the number, and I called it on three-way. A man answered. Assa introduced me to him, then instructed 2Blacc to treat me the way that he treated him. 2Blacc agreed and told me to call him back when I was off the phone with Assa. I chopped it up with the big homie for a few minutes more before he got off with me to call Ms. Bianca. I wasn't mad at him.

I didn't wanna seem thirsty, so I didn't call 2Blacc back right away, and when I did two hours later, he didn't answer. I thought I'd fucked up by not following directions, but then I received a text from him with a time and place for me to meet him later that day.

When Soldier Bag hit yo' block know I got it straight off the block / and I'ma hustle 'til it's gon' or my plug's plug run outta blocks.

Chapter 22

So, before my meeting with 2Blacc, three things happened almost at once. The first was me getting a call from Eastside Auto Body informing me that my Mercedes CL500 was ready for pickup. While on the phone with the auto shop, I received two text messages. The first was from Mack, telling me that his guy with the studio that he was talking about when we were in the County together was throwing an album release party, and he wanted me to come so he could introduce us. I was geek'd as hell, but it was the other text message that blew my fuckin' mind. It was Chrissy, telling me that she passed out at work the night before and had a follow-up doctor's appointment for the baby that she needed me to take her to. My heart kinda froze with concern, not only for the baby but for her well-being as well. My first mind told me to drop everything and rush right over to her. But then I asked myself why didn't she call me when she passed out. I wasn't stupid enough to think that she ain't been fucking anybody since we separated almost two and a half months ago. I started to text back and tell her to call that nigga, but instead, I asked how they were and what time she needed to be there.

"Aye, Loni, come take me to pick up the car. They just said it was ready!" I yelled to her from my place in front of the TV at the same time Chrissy had responded with the appointment time.

"Bae, before you hit the streets with your friends to floss yo' whip when we pick it up, can just the two of us go out and do something together?"

"You're a fuckin' mind reader. I was just 'bout to ask you if you wanted to go to this album release party with me tonight. And you kinda right about me wantin' to floss my whip when I pick it up, but it's not how you think. I gotta go meet up with Assa's guy to handle that business for him, remember?"

"Ahh, yeah, I forgot that you gotta meet with him."

"Yeah, and umm, I don't know how long it's gonna take with him. So, are we going to the party together tonight or what?" I said, parking in front of the shop. I'd already planned to use my meeting with 2Blacc as an excuse to go take Chrissy to the doctor. Loni said yes to the party. Then I convinced her to go home and start getting ready, saying that I didn't want her to see the car until I had put the rims on it. The shop had done everything already, but she didn't know that. The real reason I didn't want her to see the Benz right away was because I didn't want her to, by chance, notice Chrissy riding in it with me if we were in traffic together.

Once I was in my whip in traffic, feeling like the king of kings, I couldn't wait to see Chrissy's face when she saw my glistening Mercedes Benz CL500. I wish I would've been thinking and put on my jewelry so I could really floss on her. I wanted her to see how good I was doing without her. On the way to pick her up, I thought about everything that had happened since I last saw her. My new life was good. I pulled up in front of her apartment building and texted her to come outside. She texted back, telling me to come inside. I refused, telling her if she wasn't coming then I was leaving. Like five minutes later, she exited the building. I had the window lowered, so as soon as she spotted me, she got in the car. She wore my favorite perfume, smelling wonderful and looking just as good, dressed in an all-pink Adidas jumper that hugged her body just right. No matter what I was feeling, I didn't allow myself to cave into her seduction.

"Whose car is this?" she asked, scanning the interior.

"Mine," I said, pulling into traffic. My plan was to keep my conversation with her brief. I didn't even look at her again once she was in the car.

"Where'd you get this car from?"

"I bought it since my old one was stolen," I answered, being sarcastic. Outta the corner of my eye, I could see the hurt in her face from me giving her the cold shoulder.

"Bae, ain't nobody steal yo' car. It's right where you left it. I was tryna give it back to you today."

"Nawwwl, I think I'm good," I replied with a chuckle.

"Bae, when you coming home?"

"That ain't home for me."

"What you mean?"

"Any place I could be put out of whenever a muthafucka gets their panties in a bunch ain't home for me. That's yo' crib!"

"Don't say that! You know I didn't mean it. I miss you. We miss you," she explained, touching her belly.

"Chrissy, I'm good on you fo'real. You be treating me like a lame-ass nigga, and I keep forgiving you. I'm not gonna keep going through that shit with you or nobody else! I'll be there for my baby, but right now, I can't see shit with you." With that said, I turned up the music, and she got the point. She covered her face with her hands, crying. She sobbed for the rest of the ride to the doctor's office. I pulled in front of the entrance to let her out.

"You ain't staying?" she asked, still slightly sobbing.

"Nope, I got something to do. But here." I pulled my money outta my pocket and gave her $100. "I ain't tryna end up in jail today, and I see you in yo' body, so I think it's best that you call an Uber or something to get home." She looked like I'd just slapped her when I told her that. She got out, slammed the car door, and stomped on inside the clinic. I pulled off, laughing my ass off behind my dark-tinted windows. I was damn proud of myself. I did wonder if I'd gone too far with the reverse psychology. My hope in using that method was to get her to see that I was good with and without the help of her big brother and Maniac. And just maybe, it would help our relationship go back to what it used to be before all the bullshit.

I texted 2Blacc when I pulled up at the address over on 74th and Hampton that he'd given me and parked. He texted back, *I see you*, then I saw a super dark-complexioned guy, about six feet tall, dressed in Gucci from head to toe, get out of a lime-colored BMW 740iL sitting on 26-inch gold rims and approach my car, then get inside. He explained that he needed me to take a run with him to drop off a small knapsack that he had with him.

"Dawg, man, I like what you did with this bitch here, but let's take my whip."

"Ahh, okay," I agreed, getting out of my car and into his. He floated the BMW straight out of the state. A little over two hours later, we were parked in the back of a White Castle parking lot in the Windy City of Chicago.

"Sit tight. I'll only be a sec," 2Blacc said, then got out and walked around to the rear employee entrance of the restaurant. Moments later, it opened, and he handed the bag off to someone I couldn't see in exchange for a box. 2Blacc placed the box on the backseat of his car, got back behind the wheel, and headed back to the highway. "Bro, do you blow?"

"Nothin' but Loud."

"Shit, roll us up then," he exclaimed, reaching in the center compartment and handing me a little plastic jar of kush and a package of blunt wraps.

I rolled up, then instantly put smoke in the air. 2Blacc turned out to be cool as hell. He opened up with me more on the drive back to Milwaukee than when we left. Once we arrived back at the house on Hampton and went inside, he really started educating me on the upper level of the dope game. It was only us two in the spot because his guys were all out serving. He had me help him get the *wurk* together that he needed to get done for the day. Standing over two burners of an electric stove, he taught me how to weigh, mix, and cook up dope. I'd already learned a few tricks of the trade from watching my mom's boyfriends when I was a kid, so it wasn't hard for me to learn. When we were done, 2Blacc picked up some cash that was neatly sorted out on the pool table, counted out a couple of thousand, and gave it to me along with a cell phone.

"How do you want it—hard, soft, or both?" he asked after giving me the items.

"Let me get both. That way, if I run out of hard, I can just whip some more up," I answered, thinking about going to my mom for help getting some of the 100 ounces of powder and crack cocaine off.

"Wise man. Now, you can chop some of that down and bag it up if you want; that's on you. As long as you have my 60 racks in the end, I don't give a fuck. But that phone I gave you bangs balls, quarters, and halves like a corner boy runs through dimes. All you gotta do is answer it. The longer you keep it on, the faster you'll flip," he explained, then told me to hit him when I was done, handing $110,000 worth of product to me like it was nothing.

Chapter 23

2Blacc wasn't kidding when he said that the phone he gave moved weight like corner boys run through $10 bags. When I got in my car, I powered it on at the same time Mack texted me, asking me to ride down on him right quick about some business. I replied that I was en route to him while simultaneously answering the wildly ringing trap phone. Answering that phone 2Blacc gave me turned a 10 to 15-minute drive to go scoop up Mack into an hour-long adventure.

By the time I made it to him, I'd sold four 4½ ounce packs and three 9 pieces, making a total of 45 ounces gone. And I had a bunch of requests for eight balls and quarter ounces on standby until I could get someplace to bag some up. Thinking smartly, I stopped and purchased a box of baggies and a little digital scale before pulling up on Mack. It wasn't hard to find the address on 28th and Courtland that Mack had given me because he was chillin' on the porch of a well-kept home, talking to some females, his brother whom I recognized right away, and another unknown guy. I parked behind a 1999 Buick LeSabre with the words *For Sale* written in bold white paint on its window. My whip had immediately caught all of their attention, so I tapped the horn and lowered the window so Mack could see me. He strolled right over.

"Is this you, bro?" he asked, standing at the window.

"Yeah, this me. I just picked her up out the paint shop today," I admitted while sending calls on the trap phone to voicemail. "Aye, Mack, whose crib is that?"

"This my crib—well, me and my brother's. Why?"

"Can I go in and weigh something up right quick? I'll hit your hand."

"Hell yeah, come on. I'll tell bro to keep them outside."

When he went to tell his brother to keep their company outta the house for a minute so I could take care of business, I retrieved 7 of the remaining 55 ounces and tossed them in the bag containing the scale and baggies, then followed Mack inside the house. The inside didn't match the outside. The place was clean but damn near empty. There wasn't much furniture in it, but there was a table and chairs for me to handle my business on, and that's all I cared about.

"Good lookin' on this, bro. These muthafuckas got a nigga runnin' like crazy. That's what took me so long to get here," I explained, attempting to hand him a $50 bill.

"Man, you don't need to give me that for letting you do that. I ain't know you was doing it like this, though!"

"Shit, to be real with you, I just got out here like this. I got tired of how shit was, so I bossed up."

"Shit, I had asked you to come over here to see if you wanted to buy some screens for your car, but now I'm tryna see where I can get in with you."

"Man, if I put you on, don't make me have to touch you. I don't accept losses. You see now I don't got a problem doing shit myself, gettin' my hands dirty."

"Soldier, bro, I ain't on none of the foul shit, bro! If you put me on, I'll show you better than I can tell you. I'm tryna get up $1,200 to buy that car you parked behind. I need to catch up on the bills on this crib my grandparents left us, and some mo' shit. It's just me and Trey, so I ain't tryna get hurt or get my lil brother hurt by doin' no foul shit."

"Okay, I got you. You can start by helping me weigh and bag this here up in balls." I dumped the bag out on the glass dining room table, and Mack dived right in, helping me break down, weigh, and bag up the *wurk*. "Who selling that car out there anyway?"

"The lady next door. She just got a new lil truck. It's a runner; she kept it up. All it really needs is new tires. I got some 22s that'll go right on it."

"Check this out. This what I'ma do fo' you because once upon a time somebody did it for me. I'ma buy it for you 'cause you gonna need it fuckin' with me on this here," I said while simultaneously responding to texts on the trap phone. "I gotta go catch this money for this 9 piece before this nigga start cryin', sooo finish bagging this up for me and see if she'll take a stack for that car, and I'll be right back." I collected the ten balls we had ready, gave Mack $1,000 to get the car, then left to go catch the big money that I had waiting. I was praying that he was true to his word, but I wasn't trippin' if he ran off because I knew where he laid his head, and on top of that, from what 2Blacc had given me, I estimated that I'd make at least a $50,000 profit, so losing what I'd left Mack with wouldn't hurt what I had going on.

I returned to find Trey and his friends washing the Buick that now sat on the chrome 22s that Mack had told me about less than an hour ago. I walked in the house and found Mack right where I'd left him, only now he was hard at work at the table, breaking down an ounce of dope into crumbs. He had a burning blunt firmly between his full lips while his tattooed hands worked a razor blade with the concentration of a surgeon. A female that I didn't remember seeing the first time was seated across from him, hard at work individually bagging up the crumbs as he chopped them off.

"I see you wasn't bullshittin', my nigga. You got the rims on it already," I said, feeling a bit excited for him.

"Hell ya. Trey ass was puttin' 'em on that bitch before ole girl had the money in her hand good," Mack replied with a chuckle. "Aye, bro, I got some bread fo' you. I got off a zip and I've been runnin' through dimes like water. This shit got 'em geeking hard for it. I figured I better catch some of that bread flowing round here myself instead of lettin' them other niggas out there get it all, especially when this here better than what's over here," he explained.

"Shit, bro, that's what I'm talkin' 'bout! Let's get this shit gone!" I exclaimed, giving him a dap. I picked up a pair of latex gloves and sat down to help them. Mack introduced Trina, his female friend, to me. Trina wasn't just helping him bag up the crumbs; she was also working the back door that Mack had fiends beating down. I couldn't believe my luck. I'd gotten a plug, workers, and a jumping spot in a matter of hours. As we finished preparing the *wurk* for the streets and clearing the spot of a few of the trap phone clients who couldn't wait for me to deliver to them, I left Mack with what he had bagged in dime bags and an additional two ounces, then told him to hit me if he needed me and that I'd see him later at the party.

Then I shot back over to 2Blacc's spot with the money I owed him. We pulled up moments after each other, and I got in the car with him and handed him his money. He admitted that he was impressed. He said that he thought he wasn't going to see me until sometime the next day. I told him that I was taking a break because my girl was trippin', which was a lie. The real reason was that I wanted to get off the rest of what I still had so I had something to show for being gone all day to Loni when I got there.

"Welcome to my world," he said, laughing. "It ain't no rush with me, my nigga. I told you as long as I get mine, I'm good. So, you may as well grab this shit while you're here." I agreed, following him and the two goons with him up to the spot. Approaching the door, we saw that it had been kicked in. Somebody had broken into the house. My first thought was that they were gonna think I did it. But a neighbor told 2Blacc that it had been two guys in a car watching the spot earlier and had taken a photo of them on

152

her phone. I silently thanked God for her. 2Blacc's guy knew the car and went to handle it.

"Blacc, you want me to chill here with you 'til they get back?" I asked, wanting to show my loyalty.

"You can if you wanna see what happens to niggas that try me."

I didn't have to wait long to find that out. 2Blacc got a call, then we got in his car and went just a few blocks away to a garage. Inside, his goons had a guy on the ground crying; he pissed on himself when 2Blacc took a gun from one of his goons. He asked him why he did it and what he thought would happen when he found out. The guy admitted that he didn't think he would find out, then pleaded to be spared. Without another word, 2Blacc raised the gun and squeezed the trigger. The boom was loud as hell in the small space. It made sure I got his message loud and clear. Back at the spot, it was back to business like none of it had happened. 2Blacc gave me the same thing that he'd given me the first time and told me that he'll hit me with his new location.

I zigzagged my way to Loni's, catching sales off the trap phone along the way. It was approximately 7:30 p.m. when I pulled into the empty driveway. I let myself in the house, texting Loni to let her know I was there. She texted back that she just ran to pick them up something to eat. I told her to bring me something back, then dumped everything I had on the bed next to the outfit that she'd laid out for me to wear to the party. For some reason, becoming a dad popped in my mind, so I texted Chrissy and inquired about the doctor's visit. I was very surprised when she responded without cussing me out. She did ask me to come home again, though. I reluctantly repeated what I'd told her in the car, then wished her a good night and got in the shower.

Chapter 24

Dressed in slightly matching dark blue, cream, and burgundy Dior outfits, with our ears, neck, and wrists on bling, me and Loni weaved through the hype crowd of the album release party. At ten, when we arrived, the party was already lit. At the moment, the stage was being occupied by a local comedian who went by the name Boi Stopp.

"Babe, some dude tryna get your attention," Loni alerted me, pointing to her right. Looking in that direction, I spotted Lil Wes and Maniac approaching us.

"Wuddup, fool!" Maniac shouted excitedly, then offered me his hand to shake.

"Dawg, man, wuddup!" I replied, accepting the handshake.

"Who dis here?" Lil Wes asked, looking at Loni.

"This my friend," I answered, then turned to Loni and said, "Lady, let me holla at these fools right quick." Loni didn't protest; she simply walked off toward the bar.

"Sis told us you ridin' big boy Benz an' shit, and Realla rollin' Durango on sixes. What y'all niggas been on? Why y'all ain't been fuckin' with us?"

"Shit, I ain't know that nigga Realla was riding like that," I admitted, wondering why he ain't tell me he bought a truck. "I can't speak fo' him, but it ain't nothin' personal with me. I just been gettin' myself together." My emotions were split. On one side, I missed them, and on the other, I ain't really wanna talk to them.

"You lookin' like ya doin' that, my nigga. Aye, we need to link up an' do somethin', know what I'm sayin'?" Maniac said.

"Yeah, we can do that. My number ain't changed." Yeah, you know I had to get a jab in. They tryna make it seem like I ain't kickin' it with them when they ain't called me. "Let me go make sure shortie good though," I told them, then walked off, not giving them a chance to reply. I kinda wandered through the crowd looking for Loni. I spotted her talking to some guy in a dimly lit area. When I walked over to her, the guy was already walking off. I couldn't see his face because his back was turned.

"Hey, babe!"

"Who was that? Yo' old boyfriend or somethin'?" I inquired, surprised by my slight feeling of jealousy.

"That was my cousin."

"Aww, okay, but let me find out," I told her with a smile.

"Who were them two dudes that you didn't want me around?"

"Old friends that I ain't tryna be around myself. I really only came here to show my beautiful QB off," I said, kissing her hand. "And to holla at my guy—Mack's guy—and I did that, so let's get outta here. I been thinkin' of peeling you outta them clothes since you put 'em on."

"Is that right?" she said flirtatiously. "How 'bout you take me home, and I strip for you?"

"Even better!" With plans made, we left the party, heading back to the house. Loni wasn't playing no games. As soon as I pulled off, she dropped her head in my lap and commenced to sucking me off while I drove. I ain't never had that done before, so I was super turned on and bust quick. She swallowed it all, then sat up smiling like a cat with a mouse. I put a little more pressure on the accelerator. When we finally pulled up in the back of her house, another car immediately pulled in behind us. I looked back before putting the car in park.

"Loni, do you know who this is?"

"I never seen the car before, but it might be somebody for my mother."

As soon as I pushed the gear into park, the occupants of the car behind us got out and rushed up on my car. Instantly, I thought it was a robbery, but before I could relock the doors, my door was snatched open. I recognized the assailant's face right away. It was the same guy I beat up over the phone in the County jail. I sprung out of my seat, taking the fight to him, but he quickly drew his gun on me and shot. I didn't feel anything, so I didn't know that I'd been hit until I attempted to hit him with one of my heavy fists and dropped. He stood over me and fired twice more.

"You didn't think that I was gonna catch up with yo' bitch ass, did you!" he shouted. I grabbed my chest and felt my blood seeping out of it at the same time I heard Loni screaming.

"Don't . . . hurt her," I whispered before being overtaken by panic.

"Lady, shut the fuck up and go in the house!" I heard him shout before things went black.

The next time my eyes opened, I felt like I'd been hit by a speeding train. My entire body hurt. When my mind focused, I realized that I was in a hospital room. I tried sitting up—that's when I found that my right wrist was handcuffed to the bed rail. There was a nurse on the other side of the room not paying me any attention.

"Hey, excuse me!" I called to get his attention.

"Hi! Don't move, let me get your nurse," he said, rushing out of the room. A female nurse almost instantaneously appeared at my bedside. I think I might've briefly passed back out—I'm not sure. All I know is that she was suddenly there.

"You're awake. How do you feel?"

"I hurt everywhere."

"I bet you do. You gave us here quite a scare."

"What happened?"

"Three days ago, you were rushed here with three gunshot wounds and severe blood loss. That's all I know. Your guess is as good as mine as to why you're handcuffed."

"Three days ago? I been asleep for three days?" I repeated to myself, trying to remember the last thing I could. That's when it hit me: that dude I beat up shot me. He knew Loni's nickname. How did they know each other? From the party. That bitch set me up. That thought made my blood boil and my head pound harder. Suddenly, things went black again.

Chapter 25

Being shot ain't no joke, during or after. I can't remember a night without nightmares of that night or being snatched awake by the sound of that punk's voice saying Loni's name. Time after time, I laid drenched in sweat, grinding my teeth because of the relentless burning of the added holes in my body. I got through by plotting my revenge until the morphine drop put me out. I remember waking to the sound of my mother's angry voice around the third day I was in the hospital. She was arguing with the officer posted outside of the room. She was loud and being ghetto as ever, but I felt her love for me through the closed door. The next time the nurse came in to change my bandages, I asked why my mother wasn't allowed to see me.

"All I was told is that you're not allowed any visitors due to security reasons."

"What in the hell do they think, that my fuckin' mama shot me? That's some goofy-ass shit!"

"Daquan, I can imagine how you're feeling, but you have to try to stay calm so you won't irritate your wounds," she cautioned me. "It wouldn't help if they started bleeding again."

It was then that I found out that I wasn't even allowed to receive or make phone calls. Everyone I questioned about it fed me that same "Due to security" line. After about ten days, the doctor cleared me for release from the hospital. It was at that time that I learned I wouldn't be going home because I'd been placed in the custody of the Milwaukee Police Department. Two uniformed officers escorted me to the city jail. Neither of them shared the reason why I was going to jail; all they said was I'd know soon enough. I was placed in an interrogation room alone and told that someone would be in to talk to me shortly. I swear I must've sat in that cold-ass interview room for like four hours, missing my every-two-hour dose of pain meds twice before someone came to talk to me.

"Mr. Walker, I'm Detective Paige, and this is Detective Phillips. How are you?" Paige asked, pretending to be concerned.

"I'm confused and in fuckin' pain."

"I bet you are after being shot three times at close range," Phillips stated with a soft whistle.

"Has anyone been in to give you your pain meds?" Paige asked, looking at his notepad.

"No. Y'all the only people I seen since I was put in here."

"Well, we only have a few questions for you to answer, and we'll get you out of here so you can get something for your pain."

"Okay," I replied with a bad gut feeling about the situation I was in.

"Do you have any idea who shot you?" Phillips asked after he read me my rights to officially kick things off.

"Nope, I don't remember getting shot."

"Oh, well, your shooting isn't what we're here to talk to you about. Someone else will be in to talk to you about that when we're done. We're homicide detectives," he confessed.

Instantly, my first thought was of Loni, but then I thought of the familiar way the punk that shot me said her name and no longer felt it was her. My second thought was of the guy that 2Blacc killed in front of me. Since it was a neighbor that had ratted to 2Blacc for money, then it was probably that same neighbor that ratted to Crime Stoppers for the little reward they offered. I knew I couldn't let them see me sweat, so I put on my best game face. Detective Paige casually removed two photos from the tan legal folder that he had sitting in front of us on the table.

"Do you know either of these two guys?" he asked, showing me each photo before placing them in front of me. I was shocked to see that the photos were of the guys that me and Realla had killed in the robbery.

"Nope. Is these the muthafuckas who shot me?" I asked, faking my ignorance.

"No, remember I told you that we're not here about that."

"So, why you askin' me 'bout 'em?"

"We're asking you because you killed them!" Phillips snapped, then tossed photos of the two guys lying dead where we had left them.

"What? Y'all got me fucked up! I'm through talkin'!" I exclaimed, then just stared at the wall.

"It doesn't matter if you do or not to us. We got enough evidence to put you away for life," he threatened.

"If you got all that, what we doin' sittin' here then? Get me my meds and take me on to the County. I need a nap anyway!" I retorted. The detective stared at me in disbelief.

"Daquan, you really don't have anything you want to say? This is your chance to get out in front of this. Are you sure you don't want to talk to us?"

"I think I got a better chance at helping my situation by not saying nothin' else without a lawyer." I could see the disappointment in their faces. I chuckled, shaking my head, and watched Phillips gather the photos that were spread out on the table. With clear frustration in his voice, he told me someone would be back to get me.

After being processed through the booking room of the County jail because of my medical needs, I was exhausted by the time I made it up to Pod 5D on the fifth floor. Walking to my cell, I scanned around at all the faces of the guys staring me up and down in the day-room. The jail's intake nurse ordered that I be placed in a cell alone, which was a good thing because I wasn't healed enough to fight like that if I had to. While I was making my bed to lay down, I heard a slightly familiar voice excitedly saying my name from the doorway. I turned and was looking in the face of Assa's homeboy, Killa Rob.

"Man, wuddup!" I exclaimed, ambling over to the doorway where he stood and shook his hand.

"I see yo' young ass love jail," he said, grinning.

"Nawl, man, you know shit happens."

"Why you movin' all sluggish and shit? What's wrong with you?"

"Man, we gotta grab a seat for me to tell you all of this bullshit." We went over to a vacant table in the day-room to talk. I gave him the rundown on everything that happened to me since the last time I'd seen him. I made sure to leave out the homicides. Killa Rob was cool, but I didn't know him well enough to trust him with that information.

"So that lame got up with you and slugged you up, huh?" he said, shaking his head.

"Yeah, man, I got caught slippin'. But that bitch set me up, big bro. She had to."

"Yeah, Soldier, I don't think it's that simple, but then I don't know," he said, sounding like he wanted to say more but didn't.

"Why they move you off the pod with Assa?"

"They actually moved us both up here. You just missed him. He went up north two days ago."

"Damn!" I said, wishing I could've caught him. "How much time he get?"

"They gave big bro crazy double digits, but he finna give all that shit back on appeal though. He knew that judge was going to be on some punk shit with him. That's why he was really tryna get as much bread together as he could. He told me how you came through for him. That was some real shit."

"He actually came through for me with that. I needed that blessin' bad." Me and Killa Rob sat there choppin' it up about

161

the law and all of the dos and don'ts when faced with a homicide. He was explaining to me the difference between Felony Murder and Reckless Homicide when a guy approached us and interrupted.

"Say, my guy, somebody in the gym want you," he informed me.

"Good lookin' out," I thanked him, curious to know who wanted me. I eased over to the gymnasium's window and saw Realla. I was shocked, happy, and confused all at the same time.

"Wuddup?" I asked, throwing up my hands excitedly. He went to talking right away, but I couldn't really hear him over all the noise in the day-room. I motioned by cupping my hand around my ear to let him know that I couldn't hear him. Realla immediately held up his finger, telling me to hold on, then hastily disappeared back inside the pod that my pod shared the gymnasium with. I waited there for a little while until my body began to hurt from being on my feet so long. He was taking too long, so I'd begun walking off when he suddenly reappeared, kinda frantically knocking on the glass to get my attention. I came back, and he was sliding me a note beneath the door. I opened it right there and read it:

Soldier, I know you finna be salty at me when I tell you this, so I'ma apologize ahead of time. My bad bro, I slipped up and told my bitch about that move and she went and ran her mouth to Chrissy. I didn't know they even were kicking it with each other like that. Straight up, bro! But I made this mess we're in, so I'ma clean it up. You a real nigga, bro, you don't deserve this shit. Love, Bro!

I looked up at him, standing there looking like a sad-ass dog with his head slightly tucked. I was mad as hell. He knew better than to put serious business out there like that. I couldn't even respond or stand to keep looking at him. I just shook my head at him and walked off. I wasn't all that much

162

in panic mode about it because I'd gotten rid of my gun ASAP. Killa Rob had just finished telling me that without a weapon, all the case is, is hearsay.

"Who was that, ya guy?" Killa Rob asked when I took my seat back at the table with him.

"Yeah, something like that." I sat there holding that note, thinking about everything I'd been through. This was by far the worst. I could possibly spend the rest of my life in prison over someone else's mistake. I started to question if that detective really did have enough evidence to put me away for life. Maybe Realla made a statement. I know Chrissy has done some foul shit to me before, but I couldn't picture her doing something like turning me in on a murder. In my mind, there was no doubt that it was Realla's bitch that told. She probably found out about his lil side chick on the South Side and told to get some get-back or something like that is what I was thinking. I had gotten so upset I couldn't sit in the day-room anymore. I told Killa Rob that I had to go lay down and rest until med call, then went to the cell and laid down.

Chapter 26

The following morning is when I started losing my fuckin' mind. I tried calling Chrissy, only to learn that her number had been changed or disconnected. Knowing how she couldn't live without her phone, I knew it was off. The only other number I knew by heart was my mother's. Using the short complimentary call, I let her know how I was doing. She promised to put money on the phone for me as soon as she could, and my brother gave me his number, so I called right away using the complimentary call up on his number. After using the phone, I chilled with Killa Rob, who introduced me to his guys, Jazzy J and Nu Chainz, both about my age.

I hit it off with the two new guys right away. Jazzy J was fighting an attempted homicide, and Nu Chainz was fighting a lot of charges that came with his lifestyle as a pimp. Another day went by without me being taken to a courtroom of any kind. All of the guys said it was because the DA wasn't ready with my case yet, which meant that the evidence against me wasn't very strong. Hearing this made me feel a little better, though my heart dropped when the pod officer told me that I had an attorney visit. My limited understanding of the law had me thinking that a lawyer doesn't come see you if you're not being charged with anything.

The guy that I found waiting for me in the little conference room was new, a no-nonsense-looking guy. He sat there shuffling through a bunch of papers in his briefcase. Half holding my breath, I entered the room and sat down across from him.

"Hi, Mr. Walker, I'm Attorney Adam Scott," he introduced himself, simultaneously reaching across the table to shake my hand. "I was hired by your girlfriend to represent you in court." I happily shook his hand. I was happy for two reasons: one, I had a paid lawyer, which means that I had somebody that's going to actually fight for me, and two, the only girlfriend I had was Chrissy. I just knew she couldn't have been the one who put me in here if she got me a lawyer. "Mr. Walker, you and I have a lot to discuss, as I'm sure you know, but before we begin, your persistent and very worried girlfriend said she hasn't been able to talk to you and insisted that I call her when I came to see you so you two can talk," he explained as he retrieved his phone out of his briefcase, tapped a number on the screen, and handed the phone to me.

"Hello?" a soft female voice answered.

"Hey, wussup?" I said, smiling that I finally got to talk to Chrissy.

"Hey, babe, I miss you!" she screamed with excitement. My smile instantly turned into a frown.

"Loni?" I growled, shocked.

"Yeah, this me, who you thought it was?" she retorted in a playful manner.

"*Maaaan*, what da fuck you want!" I snapped. The lawyer looked up from his paperwork, confused by my sudden anger.

"What you mean, Daquan?"

"Bitch, don't play silly! You set me up!" I snapped.

"Nooo, baby, I didn't set you up. What you talking about?"

"Bitch, I heard dude who shot me say your name."

"That was my cousin that you seen me talkin' to at the party. I didn't know y'all knew each other, and he didn't say anything to me. I swear I didn't set you up. I'm the one who called the police." Hearing her explanation made me wanna give her the benefit of the doubt, but I was still skeptical. I had paranoid thoughts that she was only doing this because I survived. That thinking told me Loni could be just tryna cover her tracks and plotting with the punk to get a second chance at tryna kill me.

"So where that bitch-ass nigga at now?"

"I don't know. I ain't seen or heard from him since that night. I told my mother and the police what he did. I love you. I wouldn't do you like that, bae, I swear!"

"Bitch, I don't believe you!"

"Why would I get you a lawyer if I set you up?"

"What da fuck took you so long to get up with me?" I demanded.

"I never knew your last name until I got it off the title in your car. And when I tried to see you at the hospital, they wouldn't let me. You can ask your mama if you don't believe me. She was there, and they wouldn't let her in either." I knew she was telling the truth when she said that. I remembered hearing my mother arguing outside of my hospital room door. It warmed my heart hearing her say this. We talked a little more. Loni told me that she had my phone and that she'd spoken to 2Blacc and Mack. I told her to collect my money from Mack, and she told me that he'd already given her some money and told her to tell me that he's going to keep flipping what he kept and hitting her hand with my parts until I came home. The lawyer told me that I had to get off the phone. Loni promised to come see me as soon as she could. She also told me that she had put money on my books, as well as set up her phone to accept calls, and made me promise to call her.

"I love you, babe!" she confessed for the second time.

"I do too," was my reply. I ended the call feeling stupid for not saying it back and even stupider for not getting her phone number. But the lawyer wrote it down for me.

"I believe now that you two lovebirds are on the road to recovery. At least that's how it sounded to me towards the end?"

"Yeah, we're good."

"Okay, good. Now, Loni couldn't tell me anything about why you're currently being held, so how about you tell me what's going on?" Thinking fast about what Realla had written to me, I told him about how I'd broken up with Chrissy after she'd put me in jail by reporting my car stolen. I denied knowing anything about the homicides, especially when he told me that all the detectives had to go on was an anonymous tip. Recalling something that I'd just learned that day from Nu Chainz, I asked my lawyer to put in for a 90-day speedy trial.

Okay, so now you know why I'm sitting in this hellhole stressin' like I am. Especially since it's 4:40 p.m. of day 89 without a word from the courts.

"Walker!" the officer suddenly summoned me to the officer's station. As I approached, a transport officer entered the pod. Fuck! Here these muthafuckas come to get me.

"Yeah, wuddup?"

"Pack up, you've been released."

Jogging across the dayroom, I called Killa Rob over to the cell.

"Stay in touch with me. Ya know if I can do something for you, I will. All you gotta do is ask."

"All I ask is that yo' ass stay da fuck out. Slow down and live life. Think of this here as your second time at life—don't fuck it up goin' backwards."

"I won't. On everything I love, I ain't gonna go backwards. But you know, big bro, I gotta handle my business." I gave him a brotherly hug, then left. Stepping out of the thick security door that separates the jail from its lobby, I spotted three people I never would've expected to see out there waiting for me. Loni, who was pacing the floor; Mack, who looked to be mackin' on a female, and Tricc—

my brother—sitting on the bench with his eyes glued to the screen of his phone. I know now who my true friends are.

"Y'all look like y'all miss me! Wuddup!"

Yeah, I know that I got some choices to make and some loose ends to deal with that's finna really test my thuggism. But, trust me when I say that I won't be undisciplined anymore, nor will I trick myself into thinking that I'm all I got.

Soldier Bags Da Boss out!

Lock Down Publications and Ca$h Presents
Assisted Publishing Packages

Due to an increase in the price of services we have increased our prices. The prices below reflect the price increase as of 11/1/24.

BASIC PACKAGE	UPGRADED PACKAGE
$699	$1000
Editing	Typing
Cover Design	Editing
Formatting	Cover Design
	Formatting
	Upload eBooks to Amazon
	Upload Paperback to Amazon
ADVANCE PACKAGE	**LDP SUPREME PACKAGE**
$1,400	$1,700
Typing	Typing
Editing (line editing/content)	Editing (line editing/content)
Cover Design	Cover Design
Formatting	Formatting
Copyright Registration	Copyright Registration
Proofreading	Proofreading
Upload eBooks to Amazon	Set up Amazon Account
Upload Paperback to Amazon	Upload eBooks to Amazon
	Upload Paperback to Amazon
	Advertise on LDP's Amazon and Facebook Page

***Other services available upon request.
Additional charges may apply

Lock Down Publications
P.O. Box 944
Stockbridge, GA 30281-9998
Phone: 470 303-9761
Email: lockdownpublications@gmail.com

169

Submission Guideline

Submit the first three chapters of your completed manuscript to ldpsubmissions@gmail.com. In the subject line add **Your Book's Title**. The manuscript must be in a Word Doc file and sent as an attachment. Document should be in Times New Roman, double spaced, and in size 12 font. Also, provide your synopsis and full contact information. If sending multiple submissions, they must each be in a separate email.

Have a story but no way to send it electronically? You can still submit to LDP/Ca$h Presents. Send in the first three chapters, written or typed, of your completed manuscript to:

LDP: Submissions Dept
P.O. Box 944
Stockbridge, GA 30281-9998

DO NOT send original manuscript. Must be a duplicate.
Provide your synopsis and a cover letter containing your full contact information.

Thanks for considering LDP and Ca$h Presents.

NEW RELEASES

BLOODLINE OF A SAVAGE 1&2
THESE VICIOUS STREETS 1&2
RELENTLESS GOON
RELENTLESS GOON 2
BY PRINCE A. TAUHID

THE BUTTERFLY MAFIA 1-3
BY FUMIYA PAYNE

A THUG'S STREET PRINCESS 1&2
BY MEESHA

CITY OF SMOKE 2
BY MOLOTTI

STEPPERS 1,2&3
THE REAL BADDIES OF CHI-RAQ
BY KING RIO

THE LANE 1&2
BY KEN-KEN SPENCE

THUG OF SPADES 1&2
LOVE IN THE TRENCHES 2
CORNER BOYS
BY COREY ROBINSON

TIL DEATH 3
BY ARYANNA

THE BIRTH OF A GANGSTER 4
BY DELMONT PLAYER

PRODUCT OF THE STREETS 1&2
BY DEMOND "MONEY" ANDERSON

NO TIME FOR ERROR
BY KEESE

MONEY HUNGRY DEMONS
BY TRANAY ADAMS

Coming Soon from Lock Down Publications/Ca$h Presents

IF YOU CROSS ME ONCE 6
ANGEL V
By Anthony Fields

IMMA DIE BOUT MINE 5
By Aryanna

A THUGS STREET PRINCESS 3
By Meesha

PRODUCT OF THE STREETS 3
By Demond Money Anderson

CORNER BOYS 2
By Corey Robinson

THE MURDER QUEENS 6&7
By Michael Gallon

CITY OF SMOKE 3
By Molotti

CONFESSIONS OF A DOPE BOY
By Nicholas Lock

THA TAKEOVER
By Keith Chandler

BETRAYAL OF A G 2
By Ray Vinci

CRIME BOSS
By Playa Ray

Available Now

RESTRAINING ORDER 1 & 2
By **CA$H & Coffee**

LOVE KNOWS NO BOUNDARIES 1-3
By **Coffee**

RAISED AS A GOON I, II, III & IV
BRED BY THE SLUMS I, II, III
BLAST FOR ME I & II
ROTTEN TO THE CORE I II III
A BRONX TALE I, II, III
DUFFLE BAG CARTEL I II III IV V VI
HEARTLESS GOON I II III IV V
A SAVAGE DOPEBOY I II
DRUG LORDS I II III
CUTTHROAT MAFIA I II
KING OF THE TRENCHES
By **Ghost**

LAY IT DOWN I & II
LAST OF A DYING BREED I II
BLOOD STAINS OF A SHOTTA I & II III
By **Jamaica**

LOYAL TO THE GAME I II III
LIFE OF SIN I, II III
By **TJ & Jelissa**

IF LOVING HIM IS WRONG…I & II
LOVE ME EVEN WHEN IT HURTS I II III
By **Jelissa**

PUSH IT TO THE LIMIT
By **Bre' Hayes**

174

BLOODY COMMAS I & II
SKI MASK CARTEL I, II & III
KING OF NEW YORK I II, III IV V
RISE TO POWER I II III
COKE KINGS I II III IV V
BORN HEARTLESS I II III IV
KING OF THE TRAP I II
By **T.J. Edwards**

WHEN THE STREETS CLAP BACK I & II III
THE HEART OF A SAVAGE I II III IV
MONEY MAFIA I II
LOYAL TO THE SOIL I II III
By **Jibril Williams**

A DISTINGUISHED THUG STOLE MY HEART I II & III
LOVE SHOULDN'T HURT I II III IV
RENEGADE BOYS 1-4
PAID IN KARMA 1-3
SAVAGE STORMS 1-3
AN UNFORESEEN LOVE 1-3
BABY, I'M WINTERTIME COLD 1-3
A THUG'S STREET PRINCESS 1&2
By **Meesha**

A GANGSTER'S CODE 1-3
A GANGSTER'S SYN 1-3
THE SAVAGE LIFE 1-3
CHAINED TO THE STREETS 1-3
BLOOD ON THE MONEY 1-3
A GANGSTA'S PAIN 1-3
BEAUTIFUL LIES AND UGLY TRUTHS
CHURCH IN THESE STREETS
By **J-Blunt**

CUM FOR ME 1-8
An LDP Erotica Collaboration

BLOOD OF A BOSS 1-5
SHADOWS OF THE GAME
TRAP BASTARD
By **Askari**

THE STREETS BLEED MURDER 1-3
THE HEART OF A GANGSTA 1-3
By **Jerry Jackson**

WHEN A GOOD GIRL GOES BAD
By **Adrienne**

THE COST OF LOYALTY 1-3
By **Kweli**

BRIDE OF A HUSTLA 1-3
THE FETTI GIRLS 1-3
CORRUPTED BY A GANGSTA 1-4
BLINDED BY HIS LOVE
THE PRICE YOU PAY FOR LOVE 1-3
DOPE GIRL MAGIC 1-3
By **Destiny Skai**

A KINGPIN'S AMBITION
A KINGPIN'S AMBITION II
I MURDER FOR THE DOUGH
By **Ambitious**

TRUE SAVAGE 1-7
DOPE BOY MAGIC 1-3
MIDNIGHT CARTEL 1-3
CITY OF KINGZ 1&2
NIGHTMARE ON SILENT AVE
THE PLUG OF LIL MEXICO 1&2
CLASSIC CITY
By **Chris Green**

A GANGSTER'S REVENGE 1-4
THE BOSS MAN'S DAUGHTERS 1-5
A SAVAGE LOVE 1&2
BAE BELONGS TO ME 1&2
A HUSTLER'S DECEIT 1-3
WHAT BAD BITCHES DO 1-3
SOUL OF A MONSTER 1-3
KILL ZONE
A DOPE BOY'S QUEEN 1-3
TIL DEATH 1-3
IMMA DIE BOUT MINE 1-4
By **Aryanna**

A DOPEBOY'S PRAYER
By **Eddie "Wolf" Lee**

THE KING CARTEL 1-3
By **Frank Gresham**

THESE NIGGAS AIN'T LOYAL 1-3
By **Nikki Tee**

GANGSTA SHYT 1-3
By **CATO**

THE ULTIMATE BETRAYAL
By **Phoenix**

BOSS'N UP 1-3
By **Royal Nicole**

I LOVE YOU TO DEATH
By **Destiny J**

I RIDE FOR MY HITTA
I STILL RIDE FOR MY HITTA
By **Misty Holt**

LOVE & CHASIN' PAPER
By **Qay Crockett**

TO DIE IN VAIN
SINS OF A HUSTLA
By **ASAD**

BROOKLYN HUSTLAZ
By **Boogsy Morina**

BROOKLYN ON LOCK 1 & 2
By **Sonovia**

GANGSTA CITY
By **Teddy Duke**

A DRUG KING AND HIS DIAMOND 1-3
A DOPEMAN'S RICHES
HER MAN, MINE'S TOO 1&2
CASH MONEY HO'S
THE WIFEY I USED TO BE 1&2
PRETTY GIRLS DO NASTY THINGS
By **Nicole Goosby**

LIPSTICK KILLAH 1-3
CRIME OF PASSION 1-3
FRIEND OR FOE 1-3
By **Mimi**

TRAPHOUSE KING 1-3
KINGPIN KILLAZ 1-3
STREET KINGS 1&2
PAID IN BLOOD 1&2
CARTEL KILLAZ 1-3
DOPE GODS 1&2
By **Hood Rich**

THE STREETS ARE CALLING
By **Duquie Wilson**

STEADY MOBBN' 1-3
THE STREETS STAINED MY SOUL 1-3
By **Marcellus Allen**

WHO SHOT YA 1-3
SON OF A DOPE FIEND 1-4
HEAVEN GOT A GHETTO 1&2
SKI MASK MONEY 1&2
By **Renta**

GORILLAZ IN THE BAY 1-4
TEARS OF A GANGSTA 1/&2
3X KRAZY 1&2
STRAIGHT BEAST MODE 1&2
By **DE'KARI**

TRIGGADALE 1-3
MURDA WAS THE CASE 1-3
By **Elijah R. Freeman**

SLAUGHTER GANG 1-3
RUTHLESS HEART 1-3
By **Willie Slaughter**

GOD BLESS THE TRAPPERS 1-3
THESE SCANDALOUS STREETS 1-3
FEAR MY GANGSTA 1-5
THESE STREETS DON'T LOVE NOBODY 1-2
BURY ME A G 1-5
A GANGSTA'S EMPIRE 1-4
THE DOPEMAN'S BODYGAURD 1&2
THE REALEST KILLAZ 1-3
THE LAST OF THE OGS 1-3
By **Tranay Adams**

MARRIED TO A BOSS 1-3
By **Destiny Skai & Chris Green**

KINGZ OF THE GAME 1-7
CRIME BOSS 1-3
By **Playa Ray**

FUK SHYT
By **Blakk Diamond**

DON'T F#CK WITH MY HEART 1&2
By **Linnea**

ADDICTED TO THE DRAMA 1-3
IN THE ARM OF HIS BOSS
By **Jamila**

LOYALTY AIN'T PROMISED 1&2
By **Keith Williams**

YAYO 1-4
A SHOOTER'S AMBITION 1&2
BRED IN THE GAME
By **S. Allen**

TRAP GOD 1-3
RICH $AVAGE 1-3
MONEY IN THE GRAVE 1-3
CARTEL MONEY
By **Martell Troublesome Bolden**

FOREVER GANGSTA 1&2
GLOCKS ON SATIN SHEETS 1&2
By **Adrian Dulan**

TOE TAGZ 1-4
LEVELS TO THIS SHYT 1&2
IT'S JUST ME AND YOU
By **Ah'Million**

KINGPIN DREAMS 1-3
RAN OFF ON DA PLUG
By **Paper Boi Rari**

THE STREETS MADE ME 1-3
By **Larry D. Wright**

CONFESSIONS OF A GANGSTA 1-4
CONFESSIONS OF A JACKBOY 1-3
CONFESSIONS OF A HITMAN
By **Nicholas Lock**

I'M NOTHING WITHOUT HIS LOVE
SINS OF A THUG
TO THE THUG I LOVED BEFORE
A GANGSTA SAVED XMAS
IN A HUSTLER I TRUST
By **Monet Dragun**

QUIET MONEY 1-3
THUG LIFE 1-3
EXTENDED CLIP 1&2
A GANGSTA'S PARADISE
By **Trai'Quan**

CAUGHT UP IN THE LIFE 1-3
THE STREETS NEVER LET GO 1-3
By **Robert Baptiste**

NEW TO THE GAME 1-3
MONEY, MURDER & MEMORIES 1-3
By **Malik D. Rice**

CREAM 2-3
THE STREETS WILL TALK
By **Yolanda Moore**

THE STREETS WILL NEVER CLOSE 1-3
By **K'ajji**

LIFE OF A SAVAGE 1-4
A GANGSTA'S QUR'AN 1-4
MURDA SEASON 1-3
GANGLAND CARTEL 1-3
CHI'RAQ GANGSTAS 1-4
KILLERS ON ELM STREET 1-3
JACK BOYZ N DA BRONX 1-3
A DOPEBOY'S DREAM 1-3
JACK BOYS VS DOPE BOYS 1-3
COKE GIRLZ
COKE BOYS
SOSA GANG 1&2
BRONX SAVAGES
BODYMORE KINGPINS
BLOOD OF A GOON
By **Romell Tukes**

CONCRETE KILLA 1-3
VICIOUS LOYALTY 1-3
By **Kingpen**

THE ULTIMATE SACRIFICE 1-6
KHADIFI
IF YOU CROSS ME ONCE 1-3
ANGEL 1-4
IN THE BLINK OF AN EYE
By **Anthony Fields**

THE LIFE OF A HOOD STAR
By **Ca$h & Rashia Wilson**

NIGHTMARES OF A HUSTLA 1-3
BLOOD AND GAMES 1&2
By **King Dream**

GHOST MOB
By **Stilloan Robinson**

HARD AND RUTHLESS 1&2
MOB TOWN 251
THE BILLIONAIRE BENTLEYS 1-3
REAL G'S MOVE IN SILENCE
By **Von Diesel**

MOB TIES 1-7
SOUL OF A HUSTLER, HEART OF A KILLER 1-3
GORILLAZ IN THE TRENCHES
By **SayNoMore**

BODYMORE MURDERLAND 1-3
THE BIRTH OF A GANGSTER 1-4
By **Delmont Player**

FOR THE LOVE OF A BOSS 1&2
By **C. D. Blue**

KILLA KOUNTY 1-5
By **Khufu**

MOBBED UP 1-4
THE BRICK MAN 1-5
THE COCAINE PRINCESS 1-10
STEPPERS 1-3
SUPER GREMLIN 1-4
By **King Rio**

MONEY GAME 1&2
By **Smoove Dolla**

A GANGSTA'S KARMA 1-4
By **FLAME**

KING OF THE TRENCHES 1-3
By **GHOST & TRANAY ADAMS**

QUEEN OF THE ZOO 1&2
By **Black Migo**

GRIMEY WAYS 1-3
BETRAYAL OF A G
By **Ray Vinci**

XMAS WITH AN ATL SHOOTER
By **Ca$h & Destiny Skai**

KING KILLA 1&2
By **Vincent "Vitto" Holloway**

BETRAYAL OF A THUG 1&2
By **Fre$h**

THE MURDER QUEENS 1-5
By **Michael Gallon**

FOR THE LOVE OF BLOOD 1-4
By **Jamel Mitchell**

HOOD CONSIGLIERE 1&2
NO TIME FOR ERROR
By **Keese**

PROTÉGÉ OF A LEGEND 1&2
LOVE IN THE TRENCHES 1&2
By **Corey Robinson**

THE PLUG'S RUTHLESS DAUGHTER
By **Tony Daniels**

BORN IN THE GRAVE 1-3
CRIME PAYS
By **Self Made Tay**

MOAN IN MY MOUTH
By **XTASY**

TORN BETWEEN A GANGSTER AND A GENTLEMAN
By **J-BLUNT & Miss Kim**

LOYALTY IS EVERYTHING 1-3
CITY OF SMOKE 1&2
By **Molotti**

HERE TODAY GONE TOMORROW 1&2
By **Fly Rock**

WOMEN LIE MEN LIE 1-4
FIFTY SHADES OF SNOW 1-3
STACK BEFORE YOU SPLURGE
GIRLS FALL LIKE DOMINOES
NAÏVE TO THE STREETS
By **ROY MILLIGAN**

PILLOW PRINCESS
By **S. Hawkins**

THE BUTTERFLY MAFIA 1-3
SALUTE MY SAVAGERY 1&2
By **Fumiya Payne**

THE LANE 1&2
By Ken-Ken Spence

THE PUSSY TRAP 1-5
By **Nene Capri**

DIRTY DNA
By **Blaque**

SANCTIFIED AND HORNY
by **XTASY**

BOOKS BY LDP'S CEO, CA$H

TRUST IN NO MAN
TRUST IN NO MAN 2
TRUST IN NO MAN 3
BONDED BY BLOOD
SHORTY GOT A THUG
THUGS CRY
THUGS CRY 2
THUGS CRY 3
TRUST NO BITCH
TRUST NO BITCH 2
TRUST NO BITCH 3
TIL MY CASKET DROPS
RESTRAINING ORDER
RESTRAINING ORDER 2
IN LOVE WITH A CONVICT
LIFE OF A HOOD STAR
XMAS WITH AN ATL SHOOTER